Claire McGowan is the author of multiple novels in both the crime and women's fiction genres. She also writes for radio and TV, as well as being a popular teacher of creative writing. She grew up in a small village in Ireland.

Sarah Day's debut novel, *Mussolini's Island*, received a 2018 Betty Trask Award and was shortlisted for the Polari First Book Prize and the Historical Writers' Association Debut Crown. With a background in science communication, she has worked as a press officer, magazine editor and freelance writer, and was Writer in Residence at Gladstone's Library in 2019. She lives in London.

T0349294

Also by Sarah Day and Claire McGowan

Pride and Prejudice on Social Media

Jane Eyre on Social Media

Sarah Day and Claire McGowan

HODDER

First published in Great Britain in 2023 by Hodder & Stoughton
An Hachette UK company

This paperback edition published in 2023

2

Images by © Alamy
© Arcangel
© Getty
© Shutterstock
© Trevillion

A CIP catalogue record for this title is available from the British Library

Paperback ISBN 978 1 529 37019 5

Typeset by Hewer Text UK Ltd, Edinburgh
Printed and bound in Great Britain by Clays Ltd, Elcograf S.p.A.

Hodder & Stoughton policy is to use papers that are natural, renewable
and recyclable products and made from wood grown in sustainable
forests. The logging and manufacturing processes are expected to
conform to the environmental regulations of the country of origin.

Hodder & Stoughton Ltd
Carmelite House
50 Victoria Embankment
London EC4Y 0DZ

www.hodder.co.uk

Jane Eyre
on Social Media

Introduction

Within these pages you will find chronicled the life of our feisty, waifish heroine, Jane Eyre. Orphaned at birth, Jane is left in the care of her harsh Aunt Reed (not blood-related) and at age ten is sent to Lowood School, where she miraculously survives several rampant epidemics and rises to the rank of teacher (and occasional emergency trauma nurse).

Seeking out new horizons, Jane finds herself at spooky Thornfield Hall, governess to an, unfortunately French child. Her boss is hunky yet brooding, the staff are cagey, and there are some strange noises coming from the attic. (YES, so far so supermarket psych thriller. Maybe you've heard this kind of story before but trust me, you heard it here first! Miss Daphne du Maurier has a lot to answer for if you ask me.)

The following pages have been gleaned from the telephonic devices of the various dramatis personae, brought together for you now to witness the unfolding of a drama full of mystery, hardship, love, passion and triumph. For anyone who's ever been a put-upon governess, lost a loved one to an entirely preventable disease, fallen for an unavailable man or been stuck in an attic, this is for you. As a short, poor, feisty, young woman myself, I identify strongly with Jane and I'm sure you will too.

This book does for attics what *The Castle of Otranto* did for castles.

Readers who consider themselves familiar with these events may be surprised to find certain details diverge from previous accounts – don't be alarmed, truth can be subjective like that.

Readers should also be aware that in traditional fashion I have redacted some place names so as to protect the true identities of those involved – the last thing they need is a minibus full of super-fans showing up and mobbing the local tea shops. Finally, I want to stress that, although numerous attempts have been made to find deeper meaning within these pages, not everything has to be a metaphor, OK? Sometimes an attic really is just an attic.

Read on to discover the story of Jane's adventures and the mystery of Thornfield Hall.

Your correspondent,

C. Brontë

Dramatis Personae

Jane Eyre: orphan without blood relations. Independent of thought, plain of dress, miraculously immune to all known infectious diseases

At Gateshead:

The Reed family: Sarah, Jane's aunt (not by blood), her children John, Georgiana, and Eliza. Forced to take in Jane Eyre as a child owing to an unfortunate deathbed promise

Martha, Bessie: their servants

At Lowood School:

Mr Brocklehurst: the superintendent of Lowood School. What even is 'child endangerment' and 'criminal neglect'?

Miss Temple (later Mrs Temple-Nasmyth): a teacher at Lowood School

Miss Smith, Madame Pierrot, Miss Miller: teachers at Lowood School

Helen Burns: Jane's best friend at Lowood School, now deceased

Julia Severn, Mary Ann Wilson: pupils at Lowood School

At Thornfield Hall:

Edward Rochester: master of Thornfield Hall and guardian to Adèle (100 per cent not blood-related). Dashing, minted, yet inexplicably single (don't look in the attic)

Adèle Varens: his French ward. Enthusiastic about ribbons, bonnets, and cadeaux. Fortunately lacking in curiosity

Mrs Fairfax: long-suffering housekeeper at Thornfield Hall. Good at keeping secrets

Grace Poole, Leah, John, Sam, Sophie, Mary: servants at Thornfield Hall

At Marsh End:

St John Rivers: local vicar and pious do-er of good works. Hair of a Greek god, seeking female to assume missionary position

Diana and Mary Rivers: his sisters

Hannah: their servant

Other characters:

Blanche Ingram: well-ringleted socialite residing in close proximity to Thornfield Hall

The Ingram family: Blanche's mother Lady Ingram and her siblings Mary and Tedo

Rosamond Oliver: wealthy heiress residing close to Marsh End. Frequent giggler

Samuel Briggs: lawyer with knowledge of terrible secrets

Bertha Mason-Rochester: Mr Rochester's tragic first wife. RIP (don't look in the attic)

Richard Mason: her brother. Asks too many questions

In Loco Parentis

The magazine for guardians of non-blood-related orphans

In this month's issue:

The Saintly Reed Family

'We took in an ungrateful short orphan and we've only become stronger as a family': The Reed family tell all

The unexpected shock of having to raise a non-blood-related orphan hasn't held back the Reed family of Gateshead, ---shire. After a misguided promise to her husband – the juvenile delinquent's blood uncle – on his deathbed, Sarah Reed found herself saddled with an ungrateful two-week-old. Undeterred, she rolled up her sleeves and instilled a regime of gruel, discipline, and psychological warfare on the bad seed, Jane. Aided by maids Martha and Bessie, Mrs Reed ensured the criminally minded infant would never encounter dangerous indulgence or tenderness.

Said Mrs Reed, still attractive though pushing 35: 'For the good of my (blood-related) children, (son John and daughters Eliza and Georgiana) I had occasion several times to imprison her in a well-furnished apartment where she had access to occasional glasses of water and a copy of last year's almanac. You wouldn't believe the fuss she made.'

Mrs Reed recounts tales of violence and secretive book-reading: 'Aged nine she launched herself at poor John (then 14) when he found her hiding behind a curtain with a book about birds, and naturally took offence. What could I do but tie her up for hours in the room in which her uncle made his unfortunate deathbed demand?

'As she grew up she revealed her true shocking qualities of independent thought, interest in drawing, and impertinence,' said Mrs Reed, through brave tears. 'Luckily, I was able to pack her off to boarding school where she remains, despite several outbreaks of typhus, and she'll soon be eighteen and off my hands.'

Despite her ordeal, Mrs Reed remains sanguine about the experience. 'It's really brought us together as a family. In particular, it's inspired John to set up his own business and make sure he never finds himself in the embarrassing position of having to unexpectedly care for an unwanted relative. He really is an inspiration to us all.'

John's new website, www.theredroom.com, launches this week – he describes it as 'a networking and empowerment tool designed to help gentlemen achieve their greatest potential in a society where the odds are stacked against them. With some tasteful artistic depictions of the female form.'

Awwww it's eight years today since I was locked in the Red Room by my aunt and had an existential crisis that resulted in me being sent away to Lowood School! #family #japes

tagging my aunt **Sarah Reed** and dear cousins **Georgiana Reed John Reed Eliza Reed**

Jane Eyre shared a memory:

OMG I sneezed in the direction of my cousin John and now I'm locked in the Red Room again! Am so scared this room is so spooky and full of creepy mirrors, also my uncle died in here HELP

Martha Abbot
So dramatic, honestly! I seem to remember we left you in there with an Etch-a-Sketch and a couple of water biscuits

Aunt Reed
Really Jane you should be over this by now, after I took you in out of the goodness of my heart and fed and clothed you when you aren't even related to me by blood

John Reed
Typical WOMAN always complaining

Eliza Reed
This wouldn't happen in a convent

Bessie Leaven
LOL MISS JANE u r so funny xxx

Office for Standards in Children's Incarceration (OFSTINC)

Lowood School OFSTINC Report

Lowood is a thriving school based on principles of consistency and discipline. Girls are limited to one clean outfit per week, as is fitting. Meals are adequate, consisting of gruel, porridge, and water. Concerns were raised about the deaths of 34 per cent of the student body over the last year, but this is in line with government targets and no special measures are recommended.

Rating: 2.5 – Better than Workhouse

Scale:
1 Dangerously Indulgent
2 Prison
3 Workhouse
4 Actual Hell

**Madame Pierrot, Miss Smith, Jane Eyre,
Maria Temple-Nasmyth, Miss Miller**
Please report any emergencies in the 'typhus etc' group chat

Miss Smith
Hey we got 2.5 in the latest
OFSTINC report! Between Prison
and Workhouse, not bad team!

Madame Pierrot
Felicitations @JaneEyre! Eight
years today since you joined
Lowood! Not many live past five,
let alone graduate to become a
teacher here! Quelle stamina!

Maria Temple-Nasmyth
Eight whole years of typhus
outbreaks and ice in the washba-
sins but here you are

Jane Eyre
Aw thanks guys. It's been a journey.
I may be small but I'm stubbornly
resistant to most known patho-
gens. 📖 Have been thinking
though, maybe there's a world
outside Lowood? Somewhere
where dinner isn't always gruel

Madame Pierrot
Mais Jane you always love le gruel, n'est ce pas?

Miss Miller
And don't forget about Slightly Greyer Gruel Fridays! Keeps things interesting

Jane Eyre
I know I know . . . just feel I want a change, I mean I am eighteen, practically over the hill. I ask myself all the time, WWHBD? (What Would Helen Burns Do?). It's been eight years since tuberculosis carried her off before her time, seems like only yesterday she was giving me practical life advice and holding my hand during beatings

Miss Miller
Aw that's sweet. I'm pretty sure she'd tell you to be grateful for the gruel tbh

Madame Pierrot
C'est vrai, Helen really loved le gruel

Maria Temple-Nasmyth
She really did. RIP (Rest in Porridge)

Jane Eyre
@plainjane
Bio: Student, teacher, landscape painter, orphan without any blood relations. Currently teaching @lowoodschool, looking to expand my horizons

Jane Eyre @plainjane

Looking for a new position (NO JOKES PLEASE) as feel it's time to leave Lowood after eight years. Hoping I might find a governess job where I don't have to break the ice in the washstand in the mornings! Lol. Anyone know of a vacant position?

 @redroomuser385 I know a position you can vacate wink wink

> **@plainjane** What did I JUST say? Blocking

 @janefairfax Hi fellow Jane! Have you gone on **www.checkagoverness.com**? Lots of good positions on there (NO JOKES, there is nothing funny about governessing). Just keep an eye out for employers who are actually looking for wives (they're obviously the best ones to go for)

@johneyre hey, you look a lot like you might be my long-lost niece, that would be so random!! Have DMed

 @johneyre 'orphan without any blood relations' maybe not huh? 🌚

 @plainjane blocking this account

 @plainjane Witter friends, I am ONCE AGAIN warning you all against Madeiran scams, keep getting messages from some guy out there pretending to be a long-dead relative when everyone knows I am a friendless orphan, stay safe guys xxx

Posted by **AliceFairfax**

WANTED: Governess for 1 (F7) child of mysterious origins
Parentage unknown, looks absolutely nothing like her guardian, who is simply caring for her out of a deep sense of moral obligation and for the tax breaks. Candidates should be aware that the child is unfortunately French but we are doing our best to prevent it.

Posted by **TheTurnOfTheScrew**

WANTED: Governess for two (F8, M10) angelic children
100 per cent fuss-free compliance guaranteed; they are absolutely no trouble at all. They lost their former governess in a tragic accident which it would be best you never bring up.

They enjoy long walks, singing, communing with the spirit of their former governess and cross-stitch. You will need to be independent, God-fearing, and extremely incurious, especially regarding your predecessor, whom you must not bring up in conversation. (Ever). Life insurance recommended and death-in-service waiver will be requested.

Posted by **TheBanksFamily**

WANTED: All-singing all-dancing governess for two musical children
Do you break into song in unexpected moments? Do you have a cheery disposition and a smooth, well-exfoliated face? Apply now! Perfect pitch a necessity, tap and ballet experience preferred.

Posted by **CaptainVonTrapp**

WANTED: Stern no-nonsense governess for seven children
Military experience preferred
Sewing skills helpful

Religious background would be welcome
If success is achieved, promotion to matrimonial post is possible

---

Posted by **TheDarlings**

WANTED: Nanny for three London-based children. Canine preferred

---

Posted by **MaximDeWinter**

WANTED: WIFE for Cornish landowner, currently travelling in the Riviera – must not ask any questions about first wife's mysterious death

Comment /**AliceFairfax** Sir this is the governess board not the wife board

> Reply by /**MaximDeWinter** My apologies. Though I would take a governess as long as she doesn't ask too many questions

The Red Room

Prop: J. Reed Esq

**Jaded aesthetes, seducers, solipsists welcome.
Doubters, sheeple, ladies will be barred.**

Government surveillance: are they concealing their spies in new-fangled lampposts?

The King's madness: genuine affliction or health insurance scam?

REVEALED: Don Juan's top 5 tips for seduction success uncovered

'That corset makes you look thin. Are you perhaps poor and malnourished?'; Top ten negs guaranteed to work on any lady, from horny governess to haughty heiress

> **John**
> **www.theredroom.com**

> **John**
> Check it out for yourself if you're worried, no way it can fail with this kind of top content. Now will you send the PayCompanion?

Sarah
Oh dear my love, this looks rather racy

> **John**
> Come on Mum, it's not like some seedy site, it's proper investigative journalism. And dating tips. But those are based on real science

Sarah
But how does this make any money John my love?

> **John**
> Typical WOMAN always trying to stop me reaching my potential

The advice forum for aunts of wayward children

Our mission is to save doomed souls through privation, gaslighting and very plain cooking!

Glossary:

WN: wayward niece/nephew
FMBB: family member by blood
DH: disappointing husband
MW: mysterious ward

Latest posts

Re: Should I tell my WN about her FMBB?
Posted by: Aunt Reed

Some background: my much-hated WN (F18, not FMBB) lived with me for ten long, arduous years after my DH, mid-deathbed delirium, made me promise to take her in. Obviously I should have said no, but it was the end of a long and trying day, and of course you don't know a deathbed promise is a deathbed promise till after the fact do you?? Anyway, lesson learned.

Eight years ago I finally managed to get the WN into a school and away from my 2DDs and DS (Georgiana, Eliza and John, FMsBB, my darling angels) and largely forgot all about her. Easily done, she's very small and extremely plain; back in the day I quite often mistook her for a hat-stand.

We've always told her she has no family (as I've mentioned she is not a FMBB, thank God!), but a while ago I had a letter from her uncle in

Madeira, who wants to take her under his wing (clearly he's never met her, LOL). Obviously at first I suspected your typical Madeiran scam, but I looked him up and he's real, and loaded! What do I do?! Heeeeeelp. It's so unfair as I'm a bit stretched myself after giving my DS lots of money for this online periodical he's seeking investment in. Why is it the undeserving who always end up being the ones with long-lost rich relations?

Comment /**Aunt Spiker** OMG obviously you can't tell her

Reply by /**Aunt Reed** Well duh, obviously

Reply by /**Aunt Norris** Agreed, a surprise unearned inheritance is not very improving

Comment /**Aunt Lydia** If she's been at school she's v likely dead, just tell him she got typhus or something

Reply by /**Aunt Reed** THANK YOU omg can't believe I didn't think of that

www.froogle.com

Logged in: Sarah Reed

SEARCH HISTORY

Q

Am I At Fault for locking orphan niece in spooky room until she had a hallucination

Deathbed promises legally binding?

Shades of red paint Farrow and Ball

Redroom.com latest stock price

How to recoup investment from close relative (blood)

Son treatment options severe dissipation possible gonorrhoea?

From: Jane Eyre (eyrethatIbreathe@frooglemail.com)
To: Mrs Fairfax (housekeeper@thornfieldhall.com)
Date: Today at 09:43
Subject: Your Governess Advertisement

Dear Mrs Fairfax,

I am writing to apply for the position advertised, 'Governess for 1 child of mysterious origins'. Having had a slightly sketchy childhood myself I feel uniquely qualified for this exciting position. I am proficient in all the required skills mentioned, including French, drawing (examples of my humble sketches are attached), possession of a plain appearance, and the ability to become temporarily invisible in social situations as required. Hobbies include reading, fine art, independent thought, and extreme survivalism in the English countryside (this may come in handy in the event of a sudden rainstorm). Thanks to my eight years at Lowood School I am also completely immune to all known infectious diseases.

For references you may apply to Mrs Reed, my only surviving relative (not by blood), and Mr Brocklehurst, the former Superintendent of Lowood School, where I am currently a teacher/occasional emergency trauma nurse. You will note the latter's address as HMP Wormwood Scrubs – please don't be alarmed, there was just the small matter of some child neglect and death. Lowood School was rated 'Better than Workhouse' in its recent OFSTINC inspection.

Yours sincerely,

Jane Eyre, orphan

<Attached images>

From: Mrs Fairfax (housekeeper@thornfieldhall.com)
To: Jane Eyre (eyrethatIbreathe@frooglemail.com)
Date: Today at 16:42
Subject: Governess Position

Dear Miss Eyre,

I am pleased to tell you that you have been accepted for the position of governess at Thornfield Hall. You may take up the post at your earliest convenience – we just need you to complete the attached standard risk assessment and non-disclosure agreement.

Best wishes,

Alice Fairfax (Housekeeper)

Thornfield Hall Employee Risk Assessment Form

Name:

Position:

Are you prone to:

The vapours

A nervous imagination

Sleepwalking

Curiosity?

Have you ever had a hallucination within the walls of a spooky stately home? y/n

Do you have any additional skills or attributes, e.g. first aid, mild deafness, extreme credulity? Please list below:

Are you morally opposed to:

The orphans of French chorus girls

Insurance fraud

Bigamy

Living off the profits of the slave trade?

Thornfield Hall Employee NDA

Please sign here to acknowledge that you accept your charge is definitely NOT the daughter of your employer and to certify that once in post you will not attempt to enter the attic under any circumstances.

Judgement-free advice for those concerned they may be committing an impropriety

AIAF for lying about ward?

Posted by Edunderthebed

Hi all. I (M38) have recently taken my young ward (F7) to live with me, and am in the process of hiring a governess for her. I tell everyone the kid is an orphan and I care for her from the kindness of my heart, but the truth is she is starting to develop a similar hairline to me, and her mother (can-can dancer, absconded) and I did enjoy a liaison. I spat three times and turned in a circle before each encounter but recently am wondering if this is really the foolproof contraception method we've all been told it is?

Also, don't want to go into details but I'm hiding a terrible secret in the attic and it's maybe not such a good idea to bring in an outsider?

TLDR: Am I At Fault if I tell everyone my French illegitimate probable daughter is just a tragic orphaned ward I adopted, and hire a governess to work in my home which harbours a terrible secret?

Comment **/LadAboutTown** Bro what else are you supposed to do with an illegitimate kid? Don't land the rest of us in it by outing the whole 'just a tragic orphaned ward' ruse

Comment **/BaldButProud** I once hid a terrible secret in the attic and it was really bad for my hairline, don't do it

Comment **/CheesyDoesIt** Is the terrible secret in the attic a consignment of cheese you forgot about because, been there

Comment /**Sandra Gilbert and Susan Gubar** Is the terrible secret in the attic actually a metaphor though

Comment /**Bluebeard** Rookie mistake using attic, if there are any leaks your terrible secret will become v obvious, basement much better IMO

Comment /**AtticsRUs** Do you have problems with your attic such as leaks, smells, hidden family members or mice? Contact us today for a free quote

Comment /**Edunderthebed** GUYS can we please not focus on the terrible secret in the attic, not relevant, thanks

From: Jane Eyre (eyrethatIbreathe@frooglemail.com)
To: Sarah Reed (sarahreed@gateshead.net)
Date: Today at 12:52
Subject: News

Dear Aunt Reed,

Just letting you know I will be leaving Lowood soon. You know, the school you packed me off to where I almost died of typhus. But no hard feelings, it did me good in lots of ways. For example, it taught me that life is fleeting and even young children can die horribly of disease and hunger (RIP Helen), and I now have no trouble swallowing even the lumpiest of gruels. I'm pleased to say I have secured a position as a governess, so I'll be off your hands if you just give your permission. You know, seeing as I am legally your responsibility, just in case you forgot LOL.

However, I will incur some travelling expenses, so if you could find it in your kind and expansive heart to send me some money for the MegaPost, and maybe a new dress in a cheerful black, that would be great.

Hope the fam are well? I saw John's holiday shots on FB – great that he has the resources to tear it up in Margate. I enjoyed his pun about drinking 'Margs in Margs' too! Hope those 'fishbowls' don't one day lead to dissipation and fatal cirrhosis. His new website looks interesting too, I'm sure it will generate a lot of stimulating discourse (unfortunately most of the pages were blocked by my browser's miasma filter but I'm sure it's great). Georgiana looks well, I enjoy catching up with her daily recipe blog postings (several times daily in fact). And Eliza is so entertaining with her Bible quotes! It's uncanny how she always knows when I've changed my email address and manages to resubscribe me!

Lots of love,
Your niece – not by blood
Jane Eyre

www.froogle.com

Logged in: Jane Eyre

SEARCH HISTORY

Your search for: *Stately homes that weren't built on the profits of the slave trade* has returned zero results

Q   Thornfield House spooky

Legal consequences if you do not disclose a previous stress-induced hallucinatory episode

Edward Rochester love child

Peeking through the keyhole of the world's creepiest piles

Thornfield Hall

Good-sized mansion of 48 bedrooms, plus generous attic space for e.g. concealing unpalatable relatives. Stable block comes as standard, all mod cons including gas lamps, American-style larder, and cesspit.

Hill House

Featuring the only known example in the New World of independently moving corridors. Look out for messages on the walls!

Bly Manor

Ample room for an ambiguous governess, large staff, and two angelic-faced children. Grounds include a beautiful lake.

The Overlook Hotel

You can check in any time you want! Except you can't really because it's been closed due to some recent unfortunate health and safety violations.

Manderley

Cornish mansion with all mod cons (gas lamps, parquet floor, wireless), plus sailing and riding offered as standard. Needs fireproofing.

House of Usher

Come for the mysterious thumpings and bangings, stay for the atmosphere of suffocating dread.

From: John Eyre (john.eyre@madeiratraders.com)
To: Jane Eyre (eyrethatIbreathe@frooglemail.com)
Date: Today at 14:23
Subject: Long-lost relative

Dear Niece (by blood),

Resorting to email – hope this doesn't go to the tinned meat folder!
Just to let you know I've written you into my will as the sole benefi-
ciary. Can't see your Witter since you blocked me, but it looked like
you could do with the cash – not that I'm planning on popping my
clogs any time soon of course!

Anyway, I didn't want you to end up feeling like you had to enter into
exploitative employment or an unfortunate marriage of some sort
just to get by – that nest egg is all yours one day! All you need to do
is forward your current address and a couple of identifying
documents.

Your affectionate Uncle (by blood),
John Eyre

From: Jane Eyre (eyrethatIbreathe@frooglemail.com)
To: John Eyre (john.eyre@madeiratraders.com)
Date: Today at 14:48
Subject: Re: Long-lost relative

Sir, this is just becoming desperate now. Flagged as tinned meat.
So sick of these Madeiran scams!

 **Jane Eyre** Urgh these Madeiran scams are really scraping the bottom of the mead barrel now! Received another today, quite convincingly claiming to be my long-lost uncle, but luckily with my independence of thought I didn't fall for it – little does he know all my relatives are definitely dead. Beware!

 Aunt Reed Ummm yeah that's definitely a scam. I wouldn't reply, my friend Mrs Smith lost all her savings that way in a fictional sugar plantation scheme

Jane Eyre's leaving do from Lowood School

Host - Jane Eyre
6pm-late (7.30pm)
Lowood School

It seems like years since I've lived at Lowood, first as a pupil then as a teacher. So many memories – the gruel, the intermittent typhus outbreaks, the bracing indoor air . . . Come and raise a bowl of gruel with me as I move on to pastures new as a governess. I've invited all former and current teachers plus any past pupils and friends I can think of (living) but do pass on the message if I've forgotten anyone! Please mark yourself coming, not coming or dead, so I know how much gruel to get.

Alas if only our darling Helen Burns (Rest in Porridge) could join us, but I know she will be raising a gruel bowl to us from heaven! I will be giving a short forty-minute reading from *Rasselas* in her honour.

Mr Brocklehurst Very funny Miss Eyre, obviously I can't come since I'm in prison thanks to the nanny state. What even is 'child endangerment' and 'criminal neglect' anyway

Mary Ann Wilson Yeaahhhh love a gruel party, whoop whoop

Madame Pierrot J'adore le gruel anglais

 Julia Severn I'll come – since I discovered my HairMaster straighteners, my debilitating curls no longer hold me back in godly society

 Maria Temple-Nasmyth Would love to come darling Jane but since I got married four years ago I am already on my seventh pregnancy and really can't leave the Reverend Hubs with the brood

 Bessie Leaven Also preggers again but will raise a cup of No-Secco to you Miss Jane! Still remember all our fun times at Gateshead! LOL Bessie xxx

67 people cannot attend due to being dead

Jane Eyre
@plainjane
Bio: Educator, artist, world traveller (Yorkshire and a day trip to Berkshire so far), survivor. Currently governess to @orphanadele

Jane Eyre @plainjane

Excited to start my new job at Thornfield Hall today! Just a heads up – on my way from the MegaPost I bumped into a sinister-looking man who fell off his horse into a ditch. Lock your windows and doors, he had a very dark visage. Artist's impression below

Jane Eyre @plainjane

First view of Thornfield Hall! Sooo atmospheric, I couldn't help stopping for a quick sketch of the view #artist #worldtraveller

www.froogle.com

Logged in: Edward Rochester

SEARCH HISTORY

Spooky ladies in lanes

🔍 Can ladies bewitch horses

Small wan lady ankles showing

Hot ladies in lanes

The forum for tutors and governesses

Forum/newbies

Posted by PlainJane

Hi guys! First-time poster, long-time lurker here. Urgh bit nervous, starting my new job as a governess today. Found the kid's ClickClock account and here's what she said!

'Ma chère new governess starts today! Let's think of un très bon prank to welcome her properly. Should it be:

> Frogs in her shoes?
> Bleach in her porridge?
> Setting fire to her?
> N'oubliez-pas to like et comment!'

Is this normal?

Comment /**MrsWeston_néeTaylor** Hi OP, totally normal, recommend taking some antacids. Helps to drink small doses of bleach daily to wean yourself onto it

Comment /**JohnBrooke** I started keeping the frogs, they made lovely pets, and in time I even stopped hearing the ribbiting

Comment /**JaneFairfax** Hello Witter friend, good to see you here! Fire blanket is part of the uniform, you'll get the hang of it. You can get fireproof undies on MTC (**www.madeirantradingcompany.com/women's-bloomers-asbestos**)

Comment /**BeckySharp** Ignore the kid hun, keep your eyes peeled for eligible guys. Lock her in the cupboard if needs be

Comment /**WannaBMrsDeWinter**

Not a governess but companions have it hard too. If I have to fetch the gloves once I have to fetch them a hundred times

> Reply by /**MrsWeston_néeTaylor** Sympathies. Thank God my rich older husband married me and saved me from that life of servitude, I was governess to the absolute worst spoiled brat you can imagine! Still trying to get away from Emma tbh

> Reply by /**PlainJane** Oh really? That can happen then? Marrying the rich older man I mean??

> Reply by /**JaneFairfax** We're not really supposed to talk about it, check the forum rules (but yes ;))

Jane Eyre
@plainjane
Bio: Educator, artist, world traveller (Yorkshire and a day trip to Berkshire so far), survivor. Currently governess to @orphanadele

 Jane Eyre @plainjane

All settled in at Thornfield and my new job! @orphanadele you are such a sweetie! Thanks so much for the can-can welcome, let's keep it British next time, maybe a waltz or a nice salsa? Here's a pic of us in the schoolroom!

 **Jane Eyre** Well, I'm finally here! Kid is definitely going to be a handful. Seems v keen on dancing in French, talk about inappropriate. Oh – and the sinister guy with the dark visage who fell off his horse?? Only turned out to be MY BOSS. Great.

 Bessie Leaven Hahaha Miss Jane this is so you LOL xxx

 Maria Temple-Nasmyth That's actually way more awkward for him than for you, LOL

 Jane Eyre TOTALLY, he tried to come up with this lame story about how it was all my fault because I looked all spooky in the mist. So embarrassed for him

Edward, 38, looking to date 18–25 max. Craggy, grumpy, sarcastic, but absolutely minted. Widower but I don't like to talk about it so please don't look into it too closely. Guardian to Adèle who is categorically not a blood relative or French. We could honeymoon in my estates in Jamaica if you don't mind some malaria and the odd uprising.

 **FM, age varies,** looking to date human female constructed from constituent parts. Dealing with some early-life trauma, looking for companionship, understanding and revenge against my creator. Enjoys reading, walking in nature, and long Arctic hikes.

 **St John, 29,** looking to date God-fearing woman with strong constitution (immunity to malaria a plus). Enjoys travel to countries whose people would benefit from my philosophical and spiritual insights (i.e. all countries). I heard this app was good but please note I have a full head of luxurious curls, not that I care for such fripperies.

 **Maxim, 43,** widower hoping to get back on the scene so giving the apps a try! Enjoys reckless driving, sailing, costume parties. Please do not mention my dead wife. Little fools preferred.

 **Captain Von Trapp, 40,** widower suffering from an excess of offspring and an unfortunate Christian name. Naval background, enjoys discipline and order, looking for same. Women who respond to whistles preferred.

In Loco Parentis

The magazine for guardians of non-blood-related orphans

In this month's issue:

EXCLUSIVE: Her mother was tragically a can-can dancer, now she's showing tendencies – one anonymous guardian's shocking true story

QUIZ: Which governess is right for you? The replacement mother, the mysterious vamp or the potential bride?

POLL: is your governess a) seen but not heard b) not seen and not heard c) a useful hat-stand?

Mrs Fairfax, Leah, John, Mary, Grace, Sophie, Sam

Mrs Fairfax
A reminder please that the master is back today, I expect everyone to be on top form. @John, I hope the carriage has been waxed? @Mary, how's the larder looking?

Mary
We're out of gins in cans again

Grace
Nothing to do with me
But yeah get some more, strawberry flavour looks fun

Mary
Since when do you get to tell me what to order??

Grace
Er it's not for me! Need me to spell it out??

Mrs Fairfax
OK settle down. Has everyone had a chance to meet the new governess? Not adding her here for obvious reasons

John
Seems quite sweet. Incredibly plain and tiny but I guess that's all to the good, we know someone has a wandering eye . . .

Mary
So long as it's not you with the wandering eye hubs

Leah
Are we gonna tell her about . . .

Sophie
Zut alors non

Sam
Urg stop with the French will you

John
Doesn't seem like a great idea does it, bringing in new staff?

Mrs Fairfax
Everyone remembers the protocols yes?

John
Errr

Mrs Fairfax
I'll repost them. Again

Leah
Can anyone hear a weird sort of thumping sound? @Grace is that your department?

Grace
Not this time, all quiet on the top floor today. Got a new sudoku book in

Mrs Fairfax
@Sophie, I think Adèle is doing the can-can in the great hall again, can you put a stop to it please

Mary
Rarebit OK for tea again?

Grace
Goes nicely with gin that

Edward
Adèle, I've just seen your latest ClickClock. I've told you, Pilot is not having his own account, he's a dog

Adèle
🐶🐶🐶

Edward
You'll want the governess to be having one next

Adèle
She is too OLD! She uses only the Witter

Edward
What do you think of her?

Adèle
She is sweet monsieur but sooooo plain, ugh , Maman would have immediately performed 'le makeover' on her
When am I getting another cadeau btw? I want to do le unboxing for mes followers

Edward
Adèle, what is @PilottheDog doing
on ClickClock

Adèle
Look how he dances!!!

Edward
What did I JUST say

Adèle
🐾🐾🐾🐶🐶🐶

Mrs Fairfax, Leah, John, Mary, Grace, Sophie, Sam

> **Mrs Fairfax**
> Dear all, I am posting the protocols below, in case anyone needs a refresh. Updated due to presence of new governess (in hindsight that maybe wasn't such a great idea). Can everyone please read and digest?
>
> THORNFIELD HALL PROTOCOLS
> 1. Attic floor is out of bounds to all visitors and new governess
> 2. Strictly no outside visitors unless absolutely necessary
> 3. In the event of suspicious activity, our first line of defence is protocol 1: Vivid and Disturbing Dreams. Our second line of defence is protocol 2: French Cheese at Night. Protocol 3 is: Grace Poole's Alcoholism
> 4. In event of protocol 1, 2, and 3 failure, immediately activate protocol 4: Accusations of Hysteria

> **Mrs Fairfax**
> Sorry @Grace . . . but you have to admit it's not a leap

Grace
No, it's fair. We need to order in more gins in cans again btw. Just for realism's sake

John
Sorry @MrsF, regarding outside visitors, what about when Eddy invites all the poshos to toy with Miss Ingram and pretend he wants to marry her 😔

Mrs Fairfax
We'll deal with situations as and when they arise

Leah
Also can I remind everyone it's the annual laundry day on Monday so I'll need the stove all day

Sam
Yessss get in, been wearing this same shirt for eight months now

John
Ugh hate laundry day, everything smells weird afterwards. Sort of like soap instead of good old-fashioned sweat and grime

Sam
I read somewhere if you leave it
long enough your shirts clean
themselves

Lowood School

Jane Eyre Hey guys! Hope you're all doing well. Enjoying my new surroundings! Dinner last night made me think of this, who remembers??! Here we have as many as FOUR different dishes at a time, I can hardly get over it. They don't even eat gruel! (Turns out I've developed a dependency actually, if anyone knows of any decent substitutes?)

Lowood School menu for the week
Breakfast - burnt porridge
Lunch - none
Dinner - gruel, assorted
Snack - half an oatcake, subject to teacher discretion
Beverage - self-defrosted water

Mr Brocklehurst Burnt porridge never did me any harm! #snowflakes

Jane Eyre Aren't you in jail Mr B? They let you post online there? Wonder what they'd say if I dropped them a little line . . .

Mr Brocklehurst has left the group

Jane Eyre God this group is quiet, almost like a tomb lol!

Jane Eyre Sorry too soon?

Jane
Dear sir, I apologise for disturbing you

Edward
Who's that? The new governess?
Who gave you a phone?

Jane
I just wanted to raise a small
concern

Edward
They can text now! Who taught the
governesses to text?! CHRIST what is it

Jane
It's nothing really

Edward
GOD will you spit it out please

Jane
It's just I've been hearing noises
from the attic at night, like thumping sounds? Also a really weird
laugh, sort of demonic and blood-
chilling if you know what I mean?

Edward
Was it a vivid and disturbing dream?

Jane
A few of the servants suggested the same thing, funnily enough, but I don't think so, pretty sure I was awake. Also can't be cheese as I don't eat that past midday

Edward
Maybe it's rats, haha

Jane
I don't think rats thump sir. Just getting quite a weird vibe in general, and the governess hand-book says you should raise these things with your employer at the earliest opportunity, so

Edward
Is this about the thing in the lane

Jane
What thing in the— oh that

Edward
Are you some sort of witchy spooky lady, because Adèle really doesn't need that right now. Her mother was a can-can dancer you know

Jane
?

Edward
Spooky lady hanging out in a lane,
woooooooooo

Jane
It's fine never mind

Mrs Fairfax, Leah, John, Mary, Grace, Sophie, Sam

> **Mrs Fairfax**
> Look alive everyone, we may have a situation with the new governess

John
Already? I know I said he had a wandering eye but this is a new record

Leah
Gross! She's like 20 years younger than him

> **Mrs Fairfax**
> It's not that (I hope). She's been asking about strange noises from the attic. @Grace, what's going on up there?

Leah
OMG I said you were being too noisy! I mean what are you doing, Zumba?

Grace
Oh come on, what are we supposed to do, levitate? You try being stuck up there 23 hours a day, pretending to be sewing. No one's buying that btw Mrs F – as if anyone has that much sewing on the go, I mean it's not like I'm making clothes out of curtains for seven motherless children

Leah
Weirdly specific reference but OK

Mrs Fairfax
Look @Grace you're paid enough to sit around pretending to be sewing all day – and don't think I haven't seen your Etsy crochet shop, Flowers From the Attic. The least you can do is try to keep the thumping to a minimum. And what's all this about demonic laughter?

Grace
She's downloaded ClickClock. She really loves the ones of animals falling over

Mrs Fairfax
For God's sake . . . Right, can everyone just agree to stick to the protocols? The last thing we need is a repeat of last Friday's surprise visit from the insurance company

Sam
Actually I think we dealt with that very well considering

Leah
Who knew there was so much space under those floorboards?

John
What are the protocols again?

Mrs Fairfax
See above. And @Mary, can you order in some more Roquefort? We'll need it if protocol 2's going to hold up

John
I'm so confused. Which one is protocol 2 again?

Mrs Fairfax
CHEESE FFS

Mrs Fairfax
Sorry. Lost temper

Mrs Fairfax
Just – please everyone learn the protocols, situation is precarious

Mary
@John I'll explain later love

Sophie
Les anglais sont tous fous

Sam
URGH IS THAT FRENCH 🏴󠁧󠁢󠁥󠁮󠁧󠁿

www.froogle.com

Logged in: Jane Eyre

SEARCH HISTORY

Do rats thump

Hallucinations night-time noises cheese

Q   Causes of vivid and disturbing dreams

Demonic laughter water pipes sounds like

Your search for *Lowood School survivors*
has returned: zero results

The forum for tutors and governesses

Forum/spooky-stately-homes

Latest active forums:
    Marrying your boss
    Receiving unwanted pianos
    Schemes and stratagems

Weird Thumping Noises and Laughter in Attic
Posted by PlainJane

Hi guys, me again. Recently started working as a governess for a
sweet if dim and very spoiled kid (also French but in time I hope she
might forget that). My boss is old enough to be my dad but kinda hot in
a silver-fox way. Only thing is, there's this whole floor at the top of the
house I'm not supposed to go in – is that normal? Once I heard someone laughing up there. And the other night I definitely heard some sort
of strange thumping noise. I asked the servants and they said I was
probably having vivid and disturbing dreams, so maybe that's it?

Comment /RattyMcRatfacee Sounds like you have rats –
contact Hamelin Catchers for a free estimate

Comment /DeathBeforeDemocracy Have you been eating
French cheese at night? Always gives me bad dreams that our monar-
chy gets overthrown in an orgy of 'democracy'

> **Reply by /PlainJane** Yeah they suggested the cheese thing also
> but no, I only eat gruel before bed, turns out it's quite addictive

Comment /EngerlandLad If the kid's French are you sure it's not
just her doing the can-can in the attic? Heard this is quite common

Comment **/2ndMrsDeWinter** Never mind the weird thumpings, that's pretty standard – tell us more about the silver fox! Nothing wrong with an age-gap marriage babe

> Reply by **/BeckySharp** @2ndMrsDeWinter clocked your profile name-change hun, congrats!!

Comment **/FrauleinMaria** I'm kind of in the same boat here with the hot grumpy boss, let me know how that works out

> Reply by **/2ndMrsDeWinter** DM me hun xxx

Edward
What u up 2

Jane
Good morning sir. Adèle and I are practising our watercolours. We're comparing various shades of grey and black

Edward
Ha ha you are so plain and simple. Did I mention how plain you are?

Jane
You did. Might now be a good time to discuss Adèle's early years and her tendency to can-can in polite society?

Edward
Urgh must we

Jane
Or the ongoing strange attic noises? And occasional demonic laughter? Maybe I should go up there and check

Edward
OK look, I didn't want to say but there is a totally plausible explanation for all of this. I will tell you after dinner tonight

Edward
Just whatever you do don't go up there, OK?

The forum for tutors and governesses

Forum/spooky-stately-homes

Re: Weird Thumping Noises and Laughter in Attic
Posted by PlainJane

UPDATE: Hi, me again with an update to this. I had already ruled out the vivid and disturbing dreams explanation, and also cheese and rats. So my boss gave me a totally reasonable explanation for all the noises and strange happenings, which is that there's this servant who gets drunk and attacks people, but for some reason he can't fire her. He's so noble and kind, swoon! I guess it's fine and that does make sense, but all the same I can't help feeling this overbearing sense of unease and dread? Is this normal?

Comment /Anon@BlyManor Hun are you seeing faces in windows? Spooky women floating on lakes?

> **Reply by /PlainJane** Um no, why?

> > **Reply by /Anon@BlyManor** No reason! I'm so happy here with my two angels, what darlings they are. Later perhaps we shall sail toy boats on the lake

Comment /2ndMrsDeWinter God I know babe, I'm literally living this right now. Is everyone obsessed with his dead wife and saying how amazing she is and how you'll never live up?

> **Reply by /PlainJane** They don't really talk about her actually. Is that normal? I asked about her once and the housekeeper had a massive coughing fit and had to leave the room
>
>> **Reply by /2ndMrsDeWinter** Huh. Well maybe don't complain so much then

Comment /FrauleinMaria At least no one is communicating with you via whistle. It's just the one kid, right? Try seven, then come back to me

Comment /BeckySharp Enough of this worrying babes, have you got a stratagem to get your boss to propose? If not, why waste your time being a governess? You don't actually LIKE TEACHING do you??? Ha ha the very idea

Comment /JohnBrooke Does anyone need any frogs at all?

Edward
Look I hope I didn't overshare the
other night, with the whole thing
about Adèle's mum

Jane
Celine the French chorus girl who
you showered with gifts and
money? I had quite forgot

Jane
Don't worry, I get it – my cousin John
is also dissipated and has spent all
the family money founding this outra-
geously racy online periodical

Edward
Oh wow that's really shocking

Edward
Do you have a link?

Jane
www.theredroom.com

Edward
Eugh. Who would even go on such
a site?

Jane
I'm sorry to have contaminated your visage with such filth

Edward
Anyway don't go spreading the whole can-can thing about OK? It's not the kid's fault her mother was an immoral dancer and lied about Adèle's parentage

Jane
But she could be your child right?

Edward
I mean technically but I was really careful, spat three times before and turned in a circle, that's foolproof contraception as we all know

Jane
Huh

Edward
What?

Jane
Nothing sir. I meant to type 'sure'

The Red Room

Prop: J. Reed Esq

**Jaded aesthetes, seducers, solipsists welcome.
Doubters, sheeple, ladies will be barred.**

Logged in: EdwardR

The South Sea Bubble – why it was all caused by the Global Huguenot Conspiracy

Wench of the Day: saucy trollops comment on the news of the hour.
'Disraeli should stick to government instead of writing books,'
says Doris, 19, mother of four

Your recent searches:
Governess flaunts independent thought and ankles
Landowner and employee engage in egalitarian repartee
Saucy governesses in revealing black crepe
Pick-up lines governess employer age gap

Adèle
Jane

Adèle
Jane

Adèle
Jane

Adèle
Jane

Adèle
MADEMOISELLE JANE

Jane
What?? I'm busy with my watercolours. I found this new exciting shade of black to work with. It's sort of coal-coloured off-black, really vivid

Adèle
I want to show you this très cool ClickClock about le contouring. It might help you not be so, how they say, plain

Jane
You're supposed to be learning maths Adèle

Adèle
Bof! Maman never knew any maths and yet she always had plenty of money!

Jane
Yes well when you're a bit older we'll have a chat about exactly how it was Maman earned the money

Blanche, 25. Ample bosom, handsome and imposing mien. Loves: pianoforte, flirtations, costume parties. Hates: children and governesses

Georgiana, 22. Well-upholstered girl about town, ringlet game is on point, seeking minor duke or wealthy landowner to escape annoying religious maniac sister. Slide into my etchings

Eliza, 24. Mother bade me make this profile. Seeking a peaceful and godly life. If you don't pray by the hour then don't even bother, we won't get on!

Becky Sharp, 20. Listen up fellas. This is a once in a lifetime opportunity to wife a hot piece of stuff! Don't mess it up. Sharp by name and sharp by nature (like my knife LOLLLL)

Blanche Ingram's Bullet Almanac

My daily affirmations:

💜 *I dream, I believe, I receive*

💜 *A beautiful day begins with perfect ringlets*

💜 *I believe in the Mrs Rochester I am becoming*

💜 *My income, though currently static due to the patriarchy, will be limitless when I am Mrs Rochester*

💜 *I am confident in achieving my hair goals*

💜 *I place trust in my journey towards becoming Mrs Rochester*

Blanche
Hey Eds! Heard you're back at
Thornfield

Blanche
We're still just down the road if you
fancy a ride

Blanche
Hahaha I mean horse-riding
obviously

Blanche
What did you think I meant? ;)

Blanche
Is this still your number btw?

Jane
Sir. Are you abed?

Jane
It's just I can smell smoke from your chamber, are you indulging in an opium vape perhaps?

Jane
And there's that weird laughter again, you know the demonic kind

Jane
Sir?

Jane
OK I'm coming in, hope you aren't nude

Jane Eyre
@plainjane
Bio: Educator, artist, world traveller, fire safety officer. Currently
governess to @orphanadele

Jane Eyre @plainjane

IMPORTANT! Fire safety is so crucial. Last
night I was able to put out a blaze that threat-
ened to engulf my master in his sleep. Here
are some tips to avoid such a calamity:

Extinguish all sources of fire before slumber
Keep a ewer of water on hand at all times
Make sure you wake every twenty minutes
   to check no fire has taken hold
Dismiss any servants who show pyromaniac
   tendencies (I mean it's a no-brainer you
   would think)

Stay safe people!

Edward
Wow thanks very much for the wakeup call last night, so much more efficient than, I don't know, an alarm clock

Jane
My apologies sir

Jane
In my small and meagre defence, you were literally on fire

Jane
Won't happen again

Edward
Should hope not. I doubt Grace Poole will be stumbling around drunk again. I've ordered that the supply of gins in cans be monitored. Also that definitely proves it was her making those weird noises you heard. We store the cans in the attic. Case closed I guess!

Jane
It is of course none of my business sir, but is it a great idea to keep Grace Poole in the house? Just, with Adèle, and the arson and the drunkenness and everything . . .

Edward
The woman can hem a curtain in 30 seconds, you don't fire those kinds of skills. Fire! Lol, get it?

Jane
Very amusing. I mean, I could have a go at hemming. Especially considering she just burned all your bed curtains. We covered sewing at Lowood as well as reading, writing and essential deathbed nursing

Edward
Nope she stays

Jane
It just doesn't make sense. You know you could tell me if you used to have some kind of assignation with her, like with the can-can dancer? That would explain why you keep her on despite all the arson and thumping

Edward
Good God woman, Grace Poole is at least thirty-five, are you mad

Jane
Sir you are thirty-eight

Edward
UGH I FEEL SICK, THE VERY IDEA OF TOUCHING A WOMAN MY OWN AGE

Jane
OK so if you find her repugnantly old and she has a gin problem/ tendency to arson, why not fire her?

Edward
SHE STAYS

Jane
Sure, of course, makes sense . . .

From: Edward Rochester (edwardrochesteresq@thornfieldhall.com)
To: claims@reassuredgentlemen.com
Date: Today at 02:37
Subject: Unfortunate entirely accidental fire

Dear Sirs

Further to my missive of six months ago, I find myself having to
once again contact you, this time on the subject of entirely accidental fire damage. It was caused by an unfortunately deranged servant
knocking a candle onto the drapery, and is wholly unrelated to any
of my prior claims or persons named within them. Damage report is
enclosed, and swift payment would be appreciated as I have the
next instalment due on a new thoroughbred and the council tax is in
arrears (a 48-bedroom mansion doesn't come cheap amirite).

Cheers!
Ed

PS: Regarding my previous claim, reference: tragic demise, I wanted
to make you aware that payment still hasn't been received.
Apparently I need a death certificate? Something to do with tedious
English bureaucracy no doubt, wouldn't happen in the West Indies!
This is all deeply traumatic and I would appreciate swift resolution.
PayCompanion or BACS accepted.

www.froogle.com

Logged in: Jane Eyre

SEARCH HISTORY

Grace Poole dodgy past

Q Grace Poole seamstress insane

Grace Poole seamstress very plain dry skin
criminal record

Grace Poole arsonist

DRAFT MISSIVES

> **Edward**
> Hey Jane. if that even is your name,
> I hardly care enough to remember

> **Edward**
> Roses are red
> Violets are blue
> Despite your relative plainness
> I esteem you

> **Edward**
> Are you DTF (down to fraternise)

> **Edward**
> Can you come back and put out
> another fire, this one's in my LOINS

> **Edward**
> U up?

> **Edward**
> If you heard a weird noise just now
> it's probably Grace on the gin
> again. Definitely not any dark
> secret I'm hiding in the attic

Edward
Thanks for not letting me burn to death that time, that was really sweet of you

Edward
Damn girl are you a Parisian show-girl because I really want to give you all my money and

Edward
Urgh no delete

Mrs Fairfax, Leah, John, Mary, Grace, Sophie, Sam

> **Mrs Fairfax**
> You're not going to believe this

Grace
Is this about the missing gins in
cans, because that was Pilot

Mary
You're unbelievable you are

> **Mrs Fairfax**
> What? No, it's the master. In his
> infinite wisdom, he's decided now
> would be a brilliant time for a
> house party

John
WHATT???

Sophie
Zut alors, the English 🗿

Leah
Doesn't that seem a bit . . . insane?

Mrs Fairfax
I didn't say it

Leah
We're just about keeping it together with the governess in the house! I've had to use Protocol 4 three times!! She thinks we're all mad

Sam
It's like he doesn't understand the concept of a devastating secret, i.e. it's a secret know what I mean

Leah
What are we going to do??! I can't tell them all they're hysterical!

Mrs Fairfax
We may need to activate protocol 5

John
What's protocol 5??

Mrs Fairfax
Gas leak, mass hallucinations

Sam
It worked that one Christmas

John
I'm really struggling to keep up with all this

Leah
I feel like we're overlooking ghosts here? Always a v plausible explanation for weird happenings. Worked just fine in my last posting at Northanger Abbey

Mrs Fairfax
Think she's too educated to buy it. Anyway I better start putting together a shopping list for this house party. Anyone know where I can buy an inflatable dartboard? 😨

Amy, Louisa, Lady Lynn, Henry, Frederick, Mrs Colonel Dent, Sir George Lynn, Blanche, Mary, Lady Ingram, Tedo

Blanche has added Edward

Blanche
What's up party people! Can't wait for an agreeable sojourn at Thornfield Hall with our wonderful host Eddy!

Edward
Urgh please don't call me Eddy

Blanche
Fine grumps! Can we bring anything?

Edward
Um not sure, I'll get Mrs F on the caviar and WKDs and yes Henry I will order the inflatable dartboard 😶

Louisa
I'm vegan now, did I say?

Tedo

I'm on an all-gruel diet, got to get in shape for Rams! My annual trip to sunny Ramsgate that is! You know what they say, no hams before Rams

Edward

😟 Don't worry, our cook is an expert at gruel, funnily enough it seems quite popular at the moment

Blanche

Will adorable Adèle be joining us?

Edward

Probably, she likes to look at dresses and things, why?

Blanche

No reason. Can't wait to meet the darling child. I just adore children! She'll be out of the way most of the time, I suppose? A healthy 4pm bedtime is wise at her age! Which is a shame, as I just adore children

Edward

Depends on the governess I guess

Lady Ingram
There's a governess??

Edward
Well yeah, I hired one recently. If you see a very quiet and plain teenager skulking in a corner eating gruel, that's her
Why do you ask?

Lady Ingram
No reason. Love governesses, such hard-working people

Blanche, Lady Ingram, Mary, Tedo

Lady Ingram
Blanche my love, are you sure you've packed the hair curlers? You know your Amazonian bosom only looks well when set off by ringlets

Blanche
Er yeah Mum, you tell me that literally every day. Don't worry, I've got my eyes on the prize. #MrsBlancheRochester2b #manifesting

Tedo
But you don't even like him B do you?

Blanche
 He's rich! Why do I need to like him?

Lady Ingram
Well said my darling. He's rich and presentable. Well, not that presentable. But very rich

Mary
Mum will you be OK knowing there's a governess in the house?

Lady Ingram
Urgh . . . I have to be I guess

Blanche
OMG haaaaate governesses. Hate kids! Apparently she's not going to be in bed until at least 4pm

Mary
Uh huh, that kid who he's looking after out of a deep sense of obligation only

Blanche
Right, definitely not his 😏 😦

Lady Ingram
Oh well, best not to examine these things too closely. There's a stable-boy I always thought looked quite like your father. Anyway that's what boarding school is for

Blanche Ingram @blancheingramsgram

Hi followers! Are you like me, and hate heading off for a casual weekend party with a pile of luggage? I've worn out three footmen in the last year! So I was delighted when I discovered the HairMaster RingletKing. God knows I can't be seen in public with flat hair – my Amazonian bosom simply doesn't work with it. I'm offering you all 10 per cent off if you use the code AMPLE at checkout today. #hairislife #ringletking #beautifulblanche

Edward
Hi Mrs F, just wanted to give you the shopping list for the house party
75 WKDs Bubblegum Flavour
2 keggers
4 platters mixed chicken wings
18 large Domino's pizzas
More gins in cans (how are we getting through so many of these btw?)
Inflatable dartboard as discussed
And I guess your judgement on how much caviar. A barrel at least

Mrs Fairfax
Yes sir. Will Miss Jane be joining the company?

Edward
Jane? Jane who?

Edward
Oh Jane Eyre. Literally forgot she existed, definitely never think about her at all LOLLLL

Mrs Fairfax
It's just her only dresses are black, and slightly less black. Maybe she could splash out and get one in grey

Edward
Whatever you think Mrs F. Just don't forget the dartboard and make sure the delivery people know it's THORNFIELD, I keep getting the supplies for some other weekend party in Hertfordshire, I mean how many langoustines can one person handle, and it's not as if they keep

Posted by Lady Ingram

Hello again ladies. Would you believe it, am still trying to marry off my Blanche. I don't get it, she's so pretty and accomplished, yet unwed at 25. I mean, I had a nine-year-old by then. We have a good prospect with a local landowner (widowed, dodgy Caribbean past, possible love child but nbd). However we're here for the weekend hoping to seal the deal and there's some governess hanging about! I absolutely cannot stand governesses. I mean they're neither one thing nor the other – servant or person? I just like to know where I stand. I can't help but notice he seems quite distracted when she's around. What should we do? He can't possibly like the plain, weird teenage governess can he???

Comment /JaneFairfax Can't believe you are such a GEAL

> **Reply by /LadyIngram** What's a GEAL?

>> **Reply by /JaneFairfax** Governess-exclusionary aristocratic lady, look it up. Educate yourself

Amy, Louisa, Lady Lynn, Henry, Frederick, Mrs Colonel Dent, Sir George Lynn, Blanche, Mary, Lady Ingram, Tedo, Edward

Blanche
What shall we do tomorrow? This brief month-long house party is really flying by! Who's up for a costume party?

Lady Ingram
Great idea my cherub, you always look your best in flowing robes

Louisa
A tableau is always fun too!

Tedo
I'm not being the back of a horse again

Blanche
Perhaps we can persuade our noble host to serenade us?

Edward
URGH fine I'll get the Lucky Voice machine out and I guess we can do the costume thing too
Not from the attic. No one is to go near the attic, I told you that yeah?

From: orders@madeirantradingcompany.com
To: Edward Rochester (edwardrochesteresq@thornfieldhall.com)
Date: Today at 11:23
Subject: Your order is on its way

Dear Edward,

Your order of Fancy Dress Costume Sexy Fortune Teller is on its
way to: Thornfield Hall, Millcote, ---shire

Please choose a delivery option:

–leave with safe footman
–etching on delivery
–deliver to alternative mansion

Edward
But it was funny wasn't it, me dressing up as an old woman and pretending to tell your fortunes. A real jape

Jane
Not really sir, a bit offensive to the Romani community IMO
Miss Ingram was quite cast down, whatever you said to her. What did you 'see' in her future, out of interest?

Edward
Ah my little friend. Let's run away to an island together

Jane
What? Which island?

Edward
I dunno. Ibiza? Great clubs this time of year

Jane
Sigh. Whatever you say sir

Blanche
Oh hey Jean (is it Jean?), just wondered if you were joining us again tonight? Only I got enough curly straws for 12 so it will kinda throw the numbers out if so lol

Jane
I will do as my employer requests in all things Miss Ingram

Blanche
Yeah he seems to think it's good for Adèle to be in company, bless her, such a cutie, but really the best thing for her would be an early night and a boarding school. So maybe take her away sharpish after she's done showing off? Jks, love her, what a sweetie. Loved your dress last night btw, never seen that particular shade of black before

Jane
It is extremely kind of you to say so

Blanche
I think it's so good for Eddy having you around. His wife was so vivacious and fabulous, it's nice to have a bit more of a sobering presence isn't it?

Oh no I hope I haven't put my well-shod foot in it! You did know he was married?

Jane
Of course, it's in all the periodicals. So sad she died

Blanche
Abso tragic, such a loss

Jane
Oh did you meet her?

Blanche
Well no but she was in all the society papers. Absolutely stunning. I can't imagine anyone living up to her to be honest. I mean, anyone without ringlets anyway. It was such a tragedy, what happened 😨

Jane
What did happen? Wasn't clear in the articles

Blanche

Oh you don't know? LOLs, sorry, he probably only tells close friends. Surprised you didn't find it though, it has been in the periodicals. Governesses can read can't they? Like, I assume that's part of the job description? 😂 Maybe they didn't cover the story in Governesses Weekly or whatever you like to read

Here you go: **www.dailylooking-glass.com/thornfieldtragedy**

Aristocrat's Wife Dead in Tragic Canoe Accident

Bertha Mason-Rochester, beloved wife of local landowner and reformed womaniser Edward Rochester, was this morning reported drowned in her luxury canoe, which went down mysteriously last night in completely calm seas.

> 'It's absolutely baffling and of course completely devastating,' Rochester said in an interview with Raffish Rakes magazine, coincidentally already arranged for the same day. 'She was quite often inclined to pop out for a solo midnight paddle and we never had any problems before this. However, I did find a note on her pillow this morning that simply said BOY BYE so I can only conclude she was overcome by a sudden bout of feminine hysteria.'

Early reports of a woman seen tiptoeing away from the scene with a paper bag over her head whispering, 'You haven't seen anything' were later refuted by Mr Rochester, who stated, 'Most of the people who live around here are totally mad, they probably saw a stray cat or something. RIP my beautiful wife.'

Comment /MaximdeWinter Following this story with interest

Blanche Ingram @blancheingramsgram

Nothing like a spot of music is there! Wonderful evening duetting with our host and eligible bachelor @edwardrochester. Like life, singing is always better with a partner!

Use the code AMPLE to get 10 per cent off the latest innovations in pianoforte melodies

Blanche, Lady Ingram, Mary, Tedo

Lady Ingram
Urgh the governess is still here
whhhyyyy. Bringing us all down
with her black dress and plain
miserable face

Mary
Resting Governess Face

Lady Ingram
😄

Blanche
And the annoying 'ward'. I mean
hasn't he heard of orphanages? I'll
be taking care of that sharpish
once I'm Mrs Rochester

Lady Ingram
Any progress on that btw? Did he
propose while he was weirdly
dressed up as the fortune teller?

Blanche
Um. Not exactly. Bit confusing tbh

Mary
Also the annoying governess was in with him quite a while, what's that about?

Blanche
I don't KNOW, why is she even here??? URGH

Lady Ingram
Quick he's coming over phones in petticoats

Edward
Why did you go to bed so early?
Party's still going

Jane
It's past Adèle's bedtime sir

Edward
You could come back though

Jane
Oh no sir it would not be fitting I
am only a friendless orphan girl,
not to mention a governess

Edward
Well look I'm inviting you, and it's
my house

Jane
It's fine

Edward
You seemed depressed also I
noticed

Jane
I'm fine

Jane
Just, you know, there's only so
much anti-governess chat I can
take of a night
MESSAGE DELETED

From: admin@theredroom.com
To: Edward Rochester (edwardrochesteresq@thornfieldhall.com)
Date: Today at 14:56
Subject: Membership Offer

Dear Sir,

We couldn't help but notice your frequent visits to our website, and wondered if we might entice you into becoming a premium member? For a trifling fifteen guineas monthly, you can enjoy the ability to chat privately with other members, premium dating tips, and our monthly email newsletter, Red Ruminations.

Your most frequently read articles:

  Make her jealous: duet on the pianoforte with other ladies
  Top tips for proposing to household staff
  The Fake Fortune Teller Gambit: how to know what she's really
    thinking

Regards,
J. Reed Esq, proprietor

The forum for tutors and governesses

Forum/families-from-hell

Ingram family
Posted by Jane Eyre

Did anyone here ever work for the Ingram family of ---shire? Just wondering

Comment /GertietheGoverness Er yes I can tell you some tales, avoid like the plague

Comment /ShropshireLad I was a tutor to them, they literally set my shoes on fire

Comment /Idliketoteachtheworldtosing I was their governess and had to spend three years in a sanatorium to recover

Blanche Ingram @blancheingramsgram

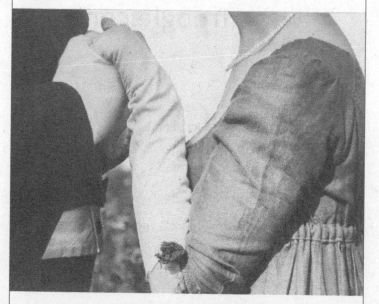

Looking for ethical diamond options, any tips lovely followers? A Certain Announcement coming your way soon ;) Can't say too much now, except he looks surprisingly hot dressed as an elderly woman telling fortunes, who knew that was a kink??? Only interested in suggestions of free-range jewel miners, thank you! #weddingbells #Ido #Iwillsayyes #whenheactuallyasksme

www.froogle.com

Logged in: Jane Eyre

SEARCH HISTORY

Blanche Ingram scandal

Blanche Ingram wears a wig

Blanche Ingram Wonderbra

Edward Rochester wife

Bertha Rochester tragic demise

Bertha Rochester death conspiracy theory paper bag

Jane
Good evening master. Just wanted to be the first to offer my congrats

Edward
What?

Jane
On your marriage? To Miss Ingram?

Edward
Ohhh that

Jane
How exciting

Edward
So you're pleased? You think it's a good idea?

Jane
It is not my place to offer an opinion. If pressed, I would perhaps venture to suggest her ringlets are artificially plump

Edward
I know! Isn't she great?

Jane
So happy for you. I'll need funds to sew Adèle some sackcloth dresses, Miss Ingram says she's sending her to boarding school 'so fast her curls will spin' and I quote

Jane
So, just let me know when I should leave and go back to tramping the roads alone

Jane
Seeing as I am a totally friendless orphan and all

Edward
You're weird

Jane
Oh no I hope I didn't put my foot in it, what am I like, just a naive orphan girl with no experience of society

Edward
BRB I hear a carriage, might be the delivery of the second inflatable dartboard, turns out there's a bit of a design flaw LOL

Mrs Fairfax, Leah, John, Mary, Grace, Sophie, Sam

Mary
Look for the last time @Sophie, we're not having frogs for dinner, I don't care if Adèle keeps putting them in your shoes. This is England not France

Sam
Urgh France

Mrs Fairfax
EMERGENCY, CODE RED TEAM WE HAVE A CODE RED

John
Sorry which one is code red?

Mrs Fairfax
Richard Mason is in the building, repeat Richard Mason is in the building

John
Oh FFS not him

Sam
The BROTHER-IN-LAW???

Mrs Fairfax
I can't help wondering if it would have made more sense to make use of the backup mansion for the purposes of discreet concealment. You only think of these things afterwards don't you?

Sam
I did suggest a moat. No one listened. It'll be fine you all said, he doesn't even have that many friends or relations. Bloody Piccadilly Circus round here

Leah
Oh my god does Richard know about . . .??

Mrs Fairfax
Of course he doesn't know, he's probably here to discuss Bertha's funeral plans. I knew that whole 'we're not holding one due to the ongoing typhus epidemic' line wouldn't work forever

Leah
Can we get rid of him??

Mrs Fairfax
@Grace now might be a good time for the old 'howling animal at night' routine

Grace
ON IT

Bertha
Hiiiiiiiii Eddy

Bertha
It's me

Bertha
Still in the attic hahaha. I know we agreed to have no contact while we wait for the insurance readies to come through, but I'm sooooo bored

Edward
Will you stop texting me while I'm with people please, if you're dead you can't exactly be posting on ClickClock can you? And while I'm on it, can you keep the noise down up there? I'm getting a lot of difficult questions about the thumping

Bertha
But I'm booooooored. And I've got to get my cardio in. Also Grace bought Twister, that's hardly my fault. When are we moving to Jamaica??

Edward
Still waiting on the life insurance money. Transfer's coming any day now, stupid banks! That wasn't you who set fire to my bedroom the other day was it???

Bertha
What, no of course not, probably a freak accident. Eddyyyyy will you bring me a Pot Noodle? Pretty please?

Edward
Look this whole scam was your idea. If you're having second thoughts . . .

Bertha
We didn't exactly have a choice! End of slavery's really messed with the finances

Bertha
Not that slavery was good! Of course not. Just, it was a bit easier on the old bank balance you have to admit. Who's that woman I keep seeing hanging around btw? The small plain one?

Edward
New governess, nbd. You know, for the kid that's definitely not mine. And she's asking a lot of questions about the noise so you and Grace need to give it a rest with the Davina McCall workout tapes, OK

Bertha
Er I'm not the one who hired an outsider! Can't believe you did that without consulting me, we're supposed to be in this together! And now you're having a house party, what were you thinking?

Edward
Got to keep up appearances. If I'm a tragically wealthy widower, the ladies are going to flock. I ain't saying she's a fortune hunter, but . . .

Bertha
Wait, I hear carriage wheels. Not another guest? OMG is that my BROTHER on the drive??! It totally is! What the hell, did you tell him I'm not actually dead?

Edward
What, no. What's he doing here? You know what, in hindsight I'm not sure this was such a watertight plan Bertha. We could have just sold your jewels or something

Mrs Fairfax, Leah, John, Mary, Grace, Sophie, Sam

Mrs Fairfax
Right. I think it's safe to say that's our biggest balls-up since the great Christmas hide-and-seek disaster. @Grace, what were you thinking??

Grace
Hang on, this is not my fault! I didn't know Richard would come looking for her stuff in the attic did I? We tried the old 'it was the ghost of your dead sister who attacked you' routine but he wasn't buying it

Mrs Fairfax
Looks like there won't be a scar at least. Miss Eyre turns out to have some fairly handy emergency nursing skills

Leah
Guess she's rumbled us now though hasn't she

Mrs Fairfax
Amazingly, I think we might actually have got away with it again. I told her it was Grace who threw the Pot Noodle. Whilst wearing a wig. And much nicer clothes. Which she found in the attic

Grace
Oh, great. So I'm an alcoholic, an arsonist, and now I'm violent. And some sort of weird attic cosplayer?

Sam
God, how dumb is Miss Eyre? I thought governesses were meant to be on the ball like

Mrs Fairfax
I did screen for credulity in the applications

Grace
I warned you. Bertha needs to get out and about. I'm telling you, she's losing it up there

Leah
Attacking her own brother though!

Grace
Look, she panicked, alright? She didn't know he'd fall backwards down the stairs. You can't blame her, have you ever tried spending time with that dude? So boring I'd stick my own head in a Pot Noodle just to avoid him

Mrs Fairfax
Just deal with the clean-up, will you?

Grace
FFS, hard enough scrubbing blue WKD out of the lounge carpet

Edward
Sooooooooooo

Edward
That was a lot

> **Jane**
> It's not a problem sir, I grew up in a typhus epidemic, so sudden and dramatic medical emergencies don't really bother me

Edward
Thanks for patching Richard up. You were really great. Sorry I had to interrupt your Love Hamlet viewing

> **Jane**
> I am at your disposal in all things sir

Edward
Oh God don't say things like that to me

> **Jane**
> What do you mean?

Jane
Master? 😉

Edward
STOPPPP

Edward
Look, aren't you just a bit curious about what happened up there?

Jane
Curiosity was specifically listed as a disqualifying characteristic in the job description sir 😉

Edward
Right. Yeah, that . . . that makes sense

Judgement-free advice for those concerned they may be committing an impropriety

AIAF for insurance scam and crush on employee?

Posted by **Edunderthebed**

A bit of background here first. I (M38) and my wife (F43 but lied about age and only allowed me to see her in very flattering lighting or I never would have obvs) had been having some financial troubles, so naturally we thought it best that she fake her death in a canoeing accident and we'd live on the insurance money in Jamaica. She's been hiding out in the attic so far, which has been pretty straightforward – I give her a decent supply of gins in cans and sudokus, and when the money comes through we shall depart for our new life together overseas. Trouble is, I'm starting to have doubts about the whole thing. We never really had much in common, and we're starting to drift apart. I know she's only just upstairs. I more mean, emotionally.

Meanwhile I hired this really plain governess (F18) to look after my 'ward' (F7, and tbqh most likely my daughter, don't rely on the 'spitting and turn-ing' method of contraception people) – in hindsight that probably wasn't that sensible given everything else going on. Governess has had some questions about the thumping etc, (think my wife might have some unre-solved anger we probably should have addressed sooner) but I think I've managed to convince her that we have a drunken pyromaniac servant, which has reassured her no end. Thing is, I've kind of fallen in love with her despite her extremely meagre appearance and am thinking of proposing? Is that mad? I mean as far as the world knows, I am a widower, so . . .

No idea what she thinks about me – I've been attempting to test her regard for me by giving her a strong impression I'm planning to marry another lady (F25, Amazonian), and the results have been inconclusive so far.

I feel like I'm not AF but getting some side-eye from the servants about it.

TLDR: Am I (M38) At Fault if I propose to my probable illegitimate daughter's governess (F18) who's half my age, when my wife (F43) is still alive and hiding out in the attic?

Comment /Faultless8457 Wow this one's going straight onto Witter

Edward Rochester
@edwardrochester
Bio: Master of Thornfield Hall, guardian to Adèle (not blood relative), world traveller, cosplayer

---

Edward Rochester @edwardrochester

When she's a Two but she:

Overlooks mysterious attic noises
Cares for a child of veiled origins
Doesn't ask too many questions about your tragic past and any secrets you may or may not be concealing in said attic

Bertha
Grace. Grace. Graaaaace come up and talk to me. I'm sooooo bored

Grace
Busy cleaning up all the Pot Noodle stains ma'am while avoiding the governess who thinks I am a murderous maniac

Bertha
Bring me a gin in a can too will you, really parched up here with nothing to do. Why did Eddy move them in the first place? Can you smuggle me a sudoku book out of the library as well?

Grace
You know, I had a job offer as a seamstress in a circus once. I could have been someone. I didn't have to end up aiding and abetting a fraud and delivering gins in cans for a living

Bertha
Oh stop moaning. You're well paid for all that 'sewing' you do (drinking gin and watching Love Hamlet)

Grace
This payout better be worth it, that's all I'm saying

The forum for men who marry their employees

Marrying the governess

Posted by EddyR

Hi lads, looking for some advice as am thinking of proposing to my ward's governess (18). She is plain and twenty years younger than me, plus completely penniless, but I can't stop thinking about her. Anyone else out there married an employee and had it work out?

Comment **/CaptainVonTrapp** I say go for it, married my governess-nun a few months back and we are very happy, plus I don't need to pay her salary anymore so it's win-win

Comment **/LordandMaster** Married my scullery maid three years ago, caused quite a stir in the community as she never knows what fish knife to use, but my floors are shining and things in the bedroom are great IYKWIM (carpets always v clean)

Comment **/MaxDW** Not my own employee but she was a 'companion' (guess anything can be called a job these days lol). It tends to work out OK so long as you don't have any dark secrets hidden in your past or anything? Good luck! (Drop me a line if you need any tips re dark secrets btw, recommend hiding them at sea rather than e.g. attics, discretion is key)

> Reply by **/EddyR** DMing you

Comment **/MrWeston** I married a governess and she is a lovely creature, intelligent and cultured, not her fault if she's in reduced circumstances. Go for it mate

The forum for men who marry their employees

Forum private messages between: EddyR and MaxDW

EddyR Disposal at sea not an option, the dark secret is my wife. Currently in the attic

MaxDW Have you considered (just an example off the top of my head) faking a boating accident?

EddyR Funny you should mention boats, we actually did that. I suppose it's a bit of a classic

MaxDW Bad luck, how did she survive? Did she have a snorkel or something?

EddyR What? No obviously I didn't actually want to kill her, it's just an insurance scam. Finances aren't what they used to be (slavery you know) so she suggested we fake her death for the money

MaxDW Oh right, of course

EddyR What were you talking about?

MaxDW Nothing

MaxDW RIP my beautiful wife

Jane Eyre
@plainjane
Bio: Educator, artist, world traveller, fire safety officer, emergency
trauma nurse. Currently governess
to @orphanadele

Jane Eyre @plainjane

When he's a Ten but he:

Dresses up as a elderly woman to trick
   you into revealing secrets
Strongly implies he's going to marry
   someone else
Has a mysteriously dead first wife

The Red Room

Prop: J. Reed Esq

**Jaded aesthetes, seducers, solipsists welcome.
Doubters, sheeple, ladies will be barred.**

New Post: the claret challenge!

Posted by: John Reed

The lying mainstream media would have us believe too much claret is damaging to our health – we all know this is LIES by Big Apothecary! In fact, many doctors RECOMMEND that you drink at least ten glasses a day to imbibe the required levels of antioxidants. To prove this, I will be drinking 8 flagons of claret in 60 seconds, after which I shall perform 100 press-ups whilst reciting the complete works of Lord Byron backwards. Join my live stream here!

 **Sarah Reed** RIP my wonderful son John. Taken too soon, through no fault of his own, in a tragic poetry-related accident. I know what the rumours are saying about him but he only drank the odd lager shandy after work and definitely wasn't dissipated in the slightest. Also I've been looking it up and there are lots of Madeiran scams about so I don't think it was even him asking me for all the money all those times. I've fallen into such a state that I will surely die soon myself, farewell to a cruel world that doesn't understand gifted and entrepreneurial young men.

 Jane Eyre So sorry to hear this Aunt Reed

 Sarah Reed Jane – will you come and see me? Kind of need to confess something before my own demise . . .

 Jane Eyre Of course I will xxx

Georgiana Reed @georgianareed

Sad times here as my dearest brother has left us and Mamma has gone into a decline. Black dress from Gateshead Tailors, mourning bonnet from Bonnet-A-Porter, gifted. Links in bio and don't forget to follow for the latest funeral updos!

@elizareed Urgh can't believe you are trying to capitalise on the death of our brother and illness of our mother. Cannot wait to get out of here and into a convent. 'For the wages of sin are death'

@georgianareed Goddd shut up judgey, I could have married a baronet you know. So sick of this family and now our dreary cousin is here too, dripping her black and grey watercolours all over the lounge! FFS

Jane Eyre Hello all, I recently found out via the deathbed confession of my aunt (not by blood) Sarah Reed (still hanging on but it's not looking good) that my uncle (by blood) John Eyre, who I always thought was dead, isn't dead at all! But now I can't find him as I blocked him on my accounts thinking it to be your usual Tinned Meat, and he seems to have deleted his.

Please share widely as I really want to connect with my one blood relative, this is nothing at all to do with his vast Madeiran riches btw.

Edward
Hey

Edward
What u up 2

Jane
Still sorting things out with my aunt
who's dying, like I said

Edward
Oh

Edward
When you coming back

Jane
Not for a while sir, she needs me

Edward
The same aunt you said was the
most heinous cow in the world and
used to lock you in scary rooms
with restraints on?

Edward
And sent you to a school where
everyone else died of typhus?

Edward
And who said your rich long-lost uncle was dead when he wasn't?

Edward
The same uncle who would have liked to adopt you and leave you his fortune?

Edward
That one?

Jane
Eh well. That's all in the past now, she hasn't got long left

Edward
You've very forgiving

Edward
That's a good thing btw

Edward
Might come in handy

Jane
What?

Edward
Nothing

The Red Room

UNDER NEW MANAGEMENT

**Jaded aesthetes, seducers, solipsists welcome.
Doubters, sheeple, ladies will be barred.**

Logged in: EdwardR

Your searches
Proposal techniques unusual
Negging proposal roundabout way

Top result

'Top 10 ways to guarantee your proposal is a success! 1: Start by
suggesting you want her to leave the country'

Jane Eyre
@plainjane
Bio: Educator, artist, world traveller, fire safety officer, emergency
trauma nurse, orphan in search of
relatives. Currently governess to
@orphanadele

Jane Eyre @plainjane

RIP my beloved Aunt Reed, we had our differ-
ences but I shall always remember you as the
woman who ensured I didn't die of exposure as
a child and fed me the basic minimum nutri-
tional intake. Not everyone would have done so
much for a poor wan orphan such as myself 1/3

Jane Eyre @plainjane

I have so much to thank her for: my extreme survivalist skills, my ability to create safe pillow forts in
any domestic space where my physical safety is
under threat, and my immunity to all known forms
of disease and intestinal parasites 2/3

Jane Eyre @plainjane

Here is a sketch of our last moments together.
It was a beautiful reconciliation, I am almost
certain the facial spasm that escaped her at

the last was an apology for all the emotional
trauma she inflicted on me as a child 🙏 3/3

 @georgianareed
Urgh she wasn't even related to you and you hated
her, stop using it for likes! Everything is so boring and
depressing here, I don't even suit black

 @elizareed
Here we go, everything has to be about
you doesn't it, even our mum and
brother dying

 @georgianareed
Like you care, St Eliza Von
Holier-than-Thou

 @plainjane
Cousins cousins! Let us hope we all
learn something from this and move
forward in the light of God's love 🙏

 @elizareed
Oh go and build a pillow fort

From: Jane Eyre (eyrethatIbreathe@frooglemail.com)
To: admin@bloodwillout.com
Date: Today at 09:26
Subject: Blood Will Out Relation Hunters

Dear Sirs,

I write to avail myself of your relation-hunting services, as I have
recently learned I have a living (blood) uncle with a considerable
fortune in Madeira. Naturally I simply want to meet my long-lost relation, the fortune is nothing to me. I hope you will be able to locate
my uncle for me as he seems to have deleted his Witter account and
my emails are bouncing (he may have had to change them after I
unfortunately reported him as a Madeiran scam, you have to be so
careful these days).

I enclose a cheek swab and look forward to hearing from you at your
earliest convenience.

Yours,
Jane Eyre

Jane
Hey, so I'm back

Edward
Who's that? Janet?

Jane
It's Jane sir

Edward
Oh yeah. Adèle will be happy her
'petite maman anglaise' is back

Jane
Aww that's sweet. So what have I
missed?

Edward
Well. You know you said I was
getting married

Jane
Yeah

Edward
Maybe you were right about that

> **Jane**
> Oh

> **Jane**
> Well congrats I suppose

Edward
You're happy?

> **Jane**
> Um not really up to me is it. When does Blanche move in?

Edward
Blanche?

> **Jane**
> Yeah your fiancée, she won't want me hanging about the place serving governess looks will she

Edward
Oh I think my new wife will be very cool with governesses 😉

> **Jane**
> What

> **Jane**
> Look I don't know what you're on about but lmk and I'll book my MegaPost out of here

Jane
Not that I have anywhere to go being alone and friendless but nbd

Edward
Where would you go Jane? I hear Ireland is nice this time of year

Jane
Sure, why not. Bit of political turmoil might liven things up

Edward
I even have a job for you

Edward
<Shared contact> Dionysius O'Gall

Jane
Is that a real person?

Edward
To be sure to be sure. She's got five daughters I hear

Jane
Right, cool

Edward
You don't want to know who my wife is going to be?

Jane
😔 Could we cut the riddles? I need to pack

Edward
Jane I will be getting married. But to you

Jane
What

Jane
What the actual hell are you talking about

Edward
I'm proposing duh

Jane
This is how you propose? By telling me you're getting married and suggesting I go to Ireland as a governess for five sisters?

Edward
I thought it was cute

Jane
God you're weird

Jane
Is this real?

> **Jane**
> I'm so confused

> **Edward**
> Yeah it's real. You're plain but what can I say, I love you

> **Edward**
> It's been really hard while you were off with your dying aunt. I missed you

> **Jane**
> Srsly?

> **Edward**
> I don't know what that means

> **Edward**
> So will you?

> **Jane**
> Are you for real?

> **Edward**
> For realz, as Adèle tells me the kids say

> **Jane**
> Oh God

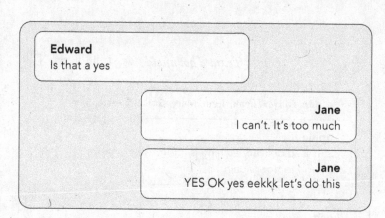

Edward
Is that a yes

Jane
I can't. It's too much

Jane
YES OK yes eekkk let's do this

Jane Eyre is now engaged to **Edward Rochester**

Team Thornfield

Mrs Fairfax, Leah, John, Mary, Grace, Sophie, Sam

Sophie
Ze missed delivery etching is through ze door again

Leah
Don't look at me! I swear no one pulled the bell pull, I was in the scullery all morning!

John
FFS, that was my horseshoes again. Three times they've tried to deliver those

Sophie
You should not order on ze Madeiran Trading Company, much better to buy at ze local artisan blacksmith

Mrs Fairfax
I DESPAIR WITH THAT MAN

Leah
What now?

Mrs Fairfax
I feel like I'm in some sort of extended hallucination. Does anyone else feel like they're in some sort of extended hallucination? Or, like they're drunk, all the time?

Grace
I know exactly what you mean

Mrs Fairfax
He's proposed to the governess

Leah
WHAT

Grace
Shots all round?

Sam
There I thought he was flirting with Miss Ingram, she's much prettier and richer and more accomplished, also taller than a small chest of drawers

Mrs Fairfax
There's no accounting for taste

Leah
I guess the ability to overlook pretty major red flags is a turn-on for him?

Mrs Fairfax
Well, she's accepted

Sam
🙈 Tell me this is an April Fool's thing

John
Sorry guys, I'm so confused

Mary
@John I'll explain later love

Leah
How exactly do we deal with this???

Mrs Fairfax
Do you know what, there isn't a protocol. I'm out. Good luck to him. Some people just can't be helped

Grace
Shots shots shots

JULY

10

Jane's Hen do!

Host - Jane Eyre
6pm-late

Jane Eyre Guys I can hardly believe this but I'm getting married! That's right, poor little plain me has only gone and snagged an aristo – he liked it so he put a ring on it! Remind me, are any of you married **Eliza Reed Georgiana Reed Blanche Ingram?** So I thought I'd organise a little hen do, nothing fancy, none of your lengthy trips to Bournemouth or pin the tail on the footman. Just some cheap wine and gruel in a few flavours. Please mark yourself going, not going, or dead

Invited: Georgiana Reed, Eliza Reed, Mary Ann Wilson, Bessie Leaven, Maria Temple-Nasmyth, Alice Fairfax, Adèle Varens, Blanche Ingram

Adèle Varens Missss can I really come! Oh ciel!

Jane Eyre You can come for the bonnet-decorating workshop but bed after that, and do try not to be quite so French dear

Bessie Leaven Sorry Miss Jane am preggers yet again but will raise some No-Secco to you! Xxx

Blanche Ingram has declined

www.noblenuptials.com

The forum for aristocratic weddings

Logged in: JaneRochester2b

Today's top articles:

Marrying a tragic widower with a past

Taking on an illegitimate 'ward'

Marrying up – your guide to using the right fork

Accidental bigamy: your guide

Marrying your cousin: from aunt to mother-in-law

Bertha
Heyyyy Eddy

Bertha
How's it going?

Bertha
Feel like I'm seeing a lot of coming and going, and also a large floral arch just got delivered? Haha it's almost like you're planning a wedding or something?

Bertha
Which would be completely mad given that you're already married and I'm very much still alive and in the attic and would also bring a lot of unnecessary attention on you just when you're trying to get the insurance money sorted for my fake death

Bertha
LOL

Bertha
Also I noticed the plain teen governess wearing a shade of slightly lighter grey and she had like a sort of half-smile on her? Anything I need to know?

Bertha
HElloooooooooooo

Bertha
EDDY WHAT'S GOING ON

Bertha
I will set fire to more than the bed so help me

Jane
Hey Mrs F, so I think we're all sorted for the wedding, I'll wear my mid-grey dress since it's a special occasion, and if you can make the gruel that should be everything

Mrs Fairfax
But madam, don't you want a veil? An amusing self-etchings booth? A dove release?

Jane
Oh no, no fuss. Maybe a small bouquet of wildflowers if they can be spared

Mrs Fairfax
But Mr R wants to buy you, and I quote 'a ton of bling'

Jane
It wouldn't be fitting for me, a poor and lowly orphan girl

Mrs Fairfax
He hasn't told you about the floral arch has he?

Jane
The what?

Mrs Fairfax
Nothing. 😕 Well I suppose no one can say you're a gold-digger love. But it's a wedding not a funeral

Jane
Alright then, maybe a gruel buffet and perhaps a small tasteful veil

Mrs Fairfax
Great

Jane
In grey

Mrs Fairfax
For God's sake. Anyway the church is booked and I've organised the honeymoon to the West Indies for you, all set so if you get away quickly then fingers crossed nothing will go horribly wrong

Jane
What do you mean?

Mrs Fairfax
Oh nothing. Don't worry

Mrs Fairfax
Lock your door maybe tonight
that's all. Also I ordered the veil in
a special non-flammable material

Jane
Er what? You're worrying me Mrs F

Mrs Fairfax
Nothing to worry about!!!!! All fine
here!!!!!!!!

www.froogle.com

SEARCH HISTORY

Legal consequences human attic concealment

Q Is it illegal to abet bigamy

Side effects of long-term attic exposure

Wedding attire fire and stabproof

Housekeeping vacancies near me

Mrs Fairfax, Leah, John, Mary, Grace, Sophie, Sam

Leah
So, just to be clear, we're not telling her about Bertha? That she's about to commit bigamy?

John
Not our problem is it

Mary
We're not abetting a crime if I organise the gruel buffet?

Grace
Honestly I don't get paid enough for this

John
You get paid more than any of us m8

Grace
Danger money for high risk of Pot Noodle-based missiles. Things can get pretty volatile up there

Leah
So what do we do? Is there a proto-col for this?

Mrs Fairfax
PROTOCOL 6, I DON'T GIVE A RAT'S ARSE

Leah
OK, that seems pretty clear

Sophie
You need ze rat's arse for ze gruel buffet? Les anglais!!!!!

Richard
Hey bro in law. Bit of a weird one but did I see that you were getting married?? Must be a mistake I know, since you're still married to my sister Bertha and all

Edward
Bertha's dead Richard, you have to let her go. And so do I. I'm moving on with my life, it's the healthy thing to do

Richard
I know what I saw in that attic

Edward
RIP my beautiful wife

Richard
Just wanted to let you know I had a really interesting chat with a Daily Looking Glass journo this morning. About . . . you know . . .

Edward
Look, I don't know what you think you saw in the attic that time, but we've got this servant called Grace who's completely bonkers. And sometimes dresses up. In my dead wife's clothes. I've been meaning to speak to her about that actually

Edward
So it was probably her. That you saw. And then you fell down the stairs in shock and hurt your head, that's all. Your sister Bertha is definitely dead, RIP, this is totally legal

Richard
Riiiiiiiiight

Edward
Anyway, who told you I was getting married?

Richard
Saw a rumour in Adequate! magazine

Edward
Mate that's barely a reputable source is it? I mean, last week they were saying corsets might be bad for women's health, as if!

Richard
Sooooo when are you getting married? Can I come? Where are you listed? Where's the honeymoon? Hear jail's lovely this time of year

Richard
HAHAHA get it? JAIL

Richard
Edward?

Richard
Hello?

www.froogle.com

Logged in: Richard Mason

SEARCH HISTORY

Society weddings this week

🔍 ---shire wedding venues

Edward Rochester engagement

Punishment for bigamy

www.froogle.com

Logged in: Jane Eyre

SEARCH HISTORY

Weird dream before wedding bad sign

Q Dreams caused by French cheese

Repairing damaged veil YouTube tutorial

Are ghosts real

The forum for tutors and governesses

Forum/spooky-stately-homes

Re: Weird Thumping Noises and Laughter in Attic
Posted by: PlainJane

GUYS oh my God someone was in my room last night. Seriously, woke up and there was this spooky figure at the end of the bed – weirdly also this overwhelming smell of Pot Noodles. Whoever it was ripped up my wedding veil, rude!! And then sprayed silly string everywhere and left a note in lipstick on the mirror that said 'bitches get stitches'?? Like, what's going on?? Is it some weird hen-do prank? I asked Hubs2be and he said it was probably either the servant Grace Poole on a bender or yet another vivid and disturbing dream – I have to be honest, both explanations are starting to wear a tad thin at this point. I don't want to sound paranoid or anything, but I think maybe there might actually be something weird going on??

Comment **/JaneFairfax** MATE we told you that six weeks ago

Comment **/Anon@BlyManor** Welcome to the same page honey

Comment **/2ndMrsDeWinter** Do you have a housekeeper? Most likely it's her being creepy, been there babe

> Reply by **/PlainJane** Mrs F? No she's so sweet, definitely not her

Comment **/JohnBrooke** Could it have been frogs? An army of frogs?

Comment **/BeckySharp** Aren't you getting hitched today?? Hun, FOCUS. EYES ON THE PRIZE

EXCLUSIVE: My sister faked her own death and hid in the attic as part of insurance scam

West Indies businessman Richard Mason (36) says he has discovered his supposedly dead sister, Bertha Rochester (43), wife of noted land-owner Edward Rochester (38), hiding in the attic of their well-appointed mansion (48 bedrooms, all mod cons). Mrs Rochester was notoriously lost in a calm sea whilst undertaking a midnight canoeing trip several months ago. Shocked entrepreneur Richard has now broken his silence to the *Daily Looking Glass*.

> 'I found her in the attic several weeks ago gorging on Pot Noodles and doing sudokus. When I confronted her, she yelled, "Oh look, a mouse!", threw the Pot Noodle at me and hid under the bed. In my shock I fell backwards down the stairs and injured myself not inconsiderably.'

Richard says he was prepared to remain silent for the sake of his sister, but couldn't keep up the charade any longer when he found out that his sister's husband, local landowner Mr Rochester, was engaged to be married to the governess (18, plain) of his ward, Adèle (French).

> 'Despite my misgivings, I kept quiet until I found out my brother-in-law was about to commit bigamy with a teenager. I'm prepared to overlook insurance fraud, the trauma of believing my sister was dead for several months, and the slightly weird situation with the kid who lives with him but apparently isn't related to him, but this was just too much.'

When confronted about his despicable acts, Edward Rochester (brooding) said, 'Well obviously I didn't think anyone would find out, did I? I merely wanted a humble, simple life with my plain yet strangely fascinating teenage girlfriend, can a man not live his dream?'

The *Daily Looking Glass* has attempted to contact Bertha Rochester for comment, but she continues to deny her own existence. An anonymous spokesperson has requested a year's supply of gins in cans in exchange for the full story.

The forum for tutors and governesses

Forum/spooky-stately-homes

Re: Weird Thumping Noises and Laughter in Attic
Posted by: PlainJane

Hey guys, me again, bit of a weird one! Probably happens more often than I think, just wondering . . . has anyone else ever found out their boss/fiancé is hiding their wife in the attic?

Comment /BeckySharp Wut

Comment /JaneFairfax Babe no

Comment /JohnBrooke That sounds like a bit of a red flag
Are you sure it isn't frogs?

Comment /Anon@BlyManor It's hard to say, I haven't seen my boss in about 6 months? I'm super happy though! Kids are absolute angels. Anyone else see weird floating heads while out for their morning stroll btw?

Comment /JaneFairfax Actual wife or are we talking elaborate fantasy situation, because honestly babe just say no

> **Reply /PlainJane** Actual wife. Supposedly dead actual wife

Comment /BeckySharp OK we were thinking the weird attic noises were a fetish thing, this is not where our private group chat theories were going

Comment /PlainJane We got as far as the church and this article pinged on my phone! I can't really marry him still.
Can I?

> **Reply /JaneFairfax** No babe. It's a crime

Comment /PlainJane He still seems optimistic about the whole thing which doesn't make much sense. I'm not the type of girl who just lives with a man, I mean what am I, a can-can dancer?

> **Reply /JaneFairfax** OK well no need to be CCDE (can-can dancer exclusionary)

Comment /2ndMrsDeWinter I was thinking he'd done something grisly to her (which btw should not be a barrier to a happy second marriage) but never imagined she was still alive! Not sure what to do with that tbh

Comment /BeckySharp Honestly you didn't even check if he was married already?? FFS hun this is amateur hour. Are you prepared to 'sort' the matter IYKWIM? 🔪

> **Reply /PlainJane** What?? No! I'd rather roam the moors alone and friendless

> **Reply /BeckySharp** 😒 At least get some cash out of him first

> **Reply /PlainJane** Extreme survivalists don't need cash. Leaving all the jewellery he gave me out on the dresser for maximum guilt-trip vibes

> **Reply /BeckySharp** You are the absolute worst at this

> **Reply /PlainJane** He thinks he's seen poor and friendless, I'll show him poor and friendless

Comment /JaneFairfax U ok hun?

Reply /PlainJane He has awoken the fell walker within

Comment /BeckySharp Should we call someone or something?

Reply /PlainJane All this girl needs is a sturdy pair of boots and some Kendal mint cake. Gonna get the late MegaPost out of here tonight and ride it till I DISAPPEAR. Then he'll be sorry

Reply /BeckySharp Or you could sue? Breach of promise, attempted bigamy, emotional distress, kinda weird child bride vibes tbh, get some cash, sell your story to the Daily Looking Glass, job's a good un?

Comment /JaneFairfax You still there babe?

This account has been deleted

Comment /BeckySharp Welp there's just no helping some people

Reply /JaneFairfax We did our best hun, she had a really chaotic vibe tbh

From: admin@bloodwillout.com
To: Jane Eyre (eyrethatIbreathe@frooglemail.com)
Date: Today at 14:53
Subject: Re: Blood Will Out Relation Hunters

Dear Miss Eyre,

Thank you for contacting us. Please find below the results of your recent DNA test. You do indeed have a living uncle (blood) and we're delighted to report you also have several first cousins living in your area!

Our search results:

The Reverend St John Rivers
Diana Rivers
Mary Rivers
Siblings residing at Marsh End Cottage, ---shire

John Eyre, residing at 1 Madeira Lane, Madeira

Yours,
www.bloodwillout.com

Relatives lost and found

www.froogle.com

Logged in: Jane Eyre

SEARCH HISTORY

Q

Where is ---shire

---shire UK directions from Thornfield Hall

---shire local amenities

St John Rivers vicar ---shire

St John Rivers
@stjohnburnz
Bio: Vicar at ---shire Parish, activist, agent of change. He/Him. Jesus is my co-coachman.

St John Rivers @stjohnburnz

Into day 14 of No-Gruel November and it's going really well. Raising money for victims of the Peterloo Massacre whilst also enjoying a healthy keto lifestyle. Please sponsor and consider doing it too!

St John Rivers @stjohnburnz

I'm doing an IronMan to raise money for victims of 'Mill Lung', please do give for this great cause!

St John Rivers @stjohnburnz

Urgh, today's article in the Daily Looking Glass is so typical of the MSM's right-wing slant – no to another South Sea bubble!

St John Rivers @stjohnburnz

@disraeli FAKE NEWS! You sir should spend more time governing and less time writing worthless 'novels' #generalelectionnow #toriesout

Diana, 24. From a good family but will be forced into governessing if I don't wed soon. Natural curls, sweet temper, just started Duolingo Hindustani!

Mary, 22. Impoverished gentlewoman with fine eyes and knowledge of German. Looking for matrimony to escape terrible fate as paid help. ---shire girl for life!

Rosamond, 19. Beautiful, rich, sweet-tempered heiress from ---shire. Always drawn to the unavailable! Le sigh. Love me, love my dog (Carlo)

St John, Diana, Mary

> **St John**
> Hey fam, just checking you've been spending your time wisely and studying your German etc.
> Hope you haven't been watching that dreadful show Love Hamlet

Diana
How could we dear brother, when you said moving pictures were the work of the devil?
Only kidding it's lots of fun reading weighty German tomes night and day

> **St John**
> Don't forget to pray several times an hour and perform good works also, it's what I do

Mary
Yes we know

Diana
Miss Oliver was round today asking for you

> **St John**
> Who?

> **St John**
> Oh Rosamond Oliver, God I forgot she existed. How is she, still flighty and spoiled I imagine?

> **Mary**
> SJ she's a totally sweetie as you know, plus her dad is minted. And she's head over heels for you for some reason 😒

> **St John**
> Whatever, I don't have time to think about it. Chop chop, once we're done with German it's time for Duolingo Hindustani

> **Mary**
> Wow can't wait

www.frooglemaps.com

Logged in: Jane Eyre

Journey options from Thornfield Hall
to Marsh End cottage, ---shire

1. Journey by private carriage with footmen:
   24 hours

2. Take the MegaPost to Whitcross, then
   wander on Moors: 2 days 15 hours

3. Take the train: 20 minutes (plus twenty
   years as not yet invented)

From: bookings@megapost.com
To: Jane Eyre (eyrethatIbreathe@frooglemail.com)
Date: Today at 22:46
Subject: You're going to The Moors!

Dear Miss Eyre,

Your MegaPost booking to The Moors is now complete. Please use the QR code to scan in on arrival and remember to take all luggage with you when you alight.

From: orders@madeirantradingcompany.com
To: Jane Eyre (eyrethatIbreathe@gmail.com)
Date: Today at 23:55
Subject: Your order is on its way!

Hi Jane,

Your Madeiran Trading Company delivery is on its way and will arrive between 01:05 and 02:05. Your order:

All-weather tent (small)
Kendal mint cake ten-pack
Woman's cagoule (black)

Please ensure a footman is available to receive your delivery, or nominate an alternative mansion.

Etching will be taken as proof of delivery.

Jane Eyre
@plainjane
Bio: Educator, artist, world traveller, fire safety officer, emergency trauma nurse, extreme survivalist. Currently between positions, throwing myself on the winds of chance

---

Jane Eyre @plainjane

OK. Deep breath. Something really weird happened to me today and I want to share it with you all. THREAD

Jane Eyre @plainjane

Tragically I have had to flee @thornfieldhall, a place of many happy memories and prior to this zero emotional trauma. Devastated to leave @orphanadele and all my cash and worldly belongings. Please don't ask for details

Jane Eyre @plainjane

I could have stayed and lived a life of riches and pleasure but I felt a higher power calling me on. Almost like my dead mother was urging me towards the light

Jane Eyre @plainjane

So, I get a @MegaPost as far as my small change allows, alight at a random crossroads and leave my bag on the coach owing to distress. At this point, I have no sustenance and barely a shawl to warm myself

Jane Eyre @plainjane

Wander alone and suffering on the moors, literally drinking from ditches (I have my Aunt Reed to thank for my lead-lined stomach, RIP). Ask a woman for some bread at one point, she says no, honestly, the cruelty of the lower-middle classes

Jane Eyre @plainjane

A small child lets me eat her burnt porridge, destined for the pigs. Thanks to my days at @lowoodschool this is a delicacy to me

Jane Eyre @plainjane

Finally, having not eaten or slept for three days, I stagger on across the moors in the wind and rain, end up collapsing on the doorstep of a random brightly-lit house, am taken in by the kind inhabitants (not blood relatives)

Jane Eyre @plainjane

Turns out I am in ---shire, a place I've never heard of or froogled before in my life, being looked after by total unrelated strangers. I have never before come across them or their names and yet they took me in. Christian charity is still alive, folks

Jane Eyre @plainjane

Conclusion: do what you know is right, even if it's hard, throw yourself to the winds of chance and you'll be fine, no risk assessments required! Thanks, Providence! (I'm living there under a pseudonym for now, needed to leave former life/boss behind.)

Jane Eyre @plainjane

My moors survival story still getting a lot of traction, if you'd like to buy me a bowl of punch click here! **www.punchme.com/ poorfriendlessjane**

 @beckysharp
Err why didn't you take any money, that was really dumb

 @bob127884
Shouldn't have left your bag on the coach should you, typical woman, so disorganised

 @SafetyFirst
This doesn't make ANY sense and tbh sounds really dangerous

 @GeographyJohn
What moors? There aren't any moors in ---shire. As a governess you ought to know the difference between a moor and a plain

@SamtheShepherd

This is fake news! OP wants us to believe she went wandering over the moors with no possessions, but I heard she had a tent, and some Kendal mint cake is clearly visible in one of her pics

 @VisitEngland

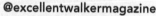---shire is beautiful this time of year, enjoy!

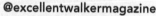 **@excellentwalkermagazine**

We'd love to talk to you more about this Jane, can you follow and DM?

The Neighbourhood Forum for Distressed Gentlefolk and Servants

---shire group

Posted by: Hannah@MarshEnd

Anyone ever had a distressed gentlewoman turn up starving on the doorstep and collapse? Seems really dodgy to me. She's not so weak she hasn't already eaten all the Coco Pops and I found a Madeiran Trading Company alert on her phone for a new cagoule, plus her pockets were full of Kendal mint cake wrappers. But my mistresses are totally taken in and want to let her recover here while she eats us out of Coco Pops. I've tried being hostile and muttering but it's not working.

Comment **/NellyDean** God these poshos really are dim sometimes. I've got mine wailing and bashing at the windows all hours, almost out of Windex wiping away all the handprints, so solidarity babe

Comment **/MarianneDashwood** Perhaps she has suffered a romantic disappointment and got lost in a rain shower? Let us be charitable

Comment **/JaneBennet** It happens, a near-fatal cold can be contracted in even a light sprinkling of rain. Was she on horseback by any chance?

Diana, Mary, St John

> **St John**
> Who is this random woman you've taken in? Is she 'poor' poor, or deserving poor? Or another gentlewoman lost on a hen do?

> **Mary**
> We don't know dummy, she's out cold!

> **St John**
> Check her hands for indications of gentleness

> **Diana**
> She ate a lot of Coco Pops earlier, they're probably too refined for undeserving stomachs?

> **Mary**
> I think she mumbled something in French, sounded like 'Adèle, come down from the chandelier'?

St John
Shame it wasn't German, but still, she's clearly literate, and she knows what a chandelier is

Diana
What's that got to do with anything?

St John
What about her visage – comely or not comely?

Mary
St John!!

St John
I merely seek indications of her status. Have you checked her ankles?

Mary
Signing out now

> **Mary**
> Poor thing, can barely manage
> Coco Pops

Diana
I know, out on the moors starving
and friendless. It's so sad

> **Mary**
> Weird how he's all sympathy for the
> grubby urchins hereabouts but not
> for a clever and gentle lady who
> collapses on our doorstep, isn't it

> **Mary**
> Almost like he has a thing against
> cultured young women?

Diana
THANK YOU at last someone said
it

The Red Room

UNDER NEW
MANAGEMENT

**Jaded aesthetes, seducers, solipsists welcome.
Doubters, sheeple, ladies will be barred.**

Logged in: St John Rivers

Your searches
    Sexy mill owner's daughter yields to Marxist dialectic
    Vicar chastises upper-class lady, sees her ankles
    Mill owner's daughter enjoys missionary (work in India)

Rosamond
Oh hi SJ, how are you today? Just dropping you a line to say hello. Do you like these new shoes I bought?

St John
Rosamond I can almost see your ankles in that engraving! For shame

Rosamond
Oh whoops tee-hee. You like them? The shoes that is . . .

St John
Very pretty but let's remember some people don't even have feet yeah?

Rosamond
☹ Are you coming round to see Pops today?

St John
No I have much more important things to do like visiting orphans and the sick. I don't have time for FRIPPERY Rosamond

St John
Did you read those tracts I sent you btw?

Rosamond
I glanced at them

St John
Sigh

Rosamond
There were a lot of words SJ and no engravings, also I'm behind on my viewing of Love Hamlet

Rosamond
What's going on with your extremely plain new friend btw?

St John
Oh Jane Elliot, as she calls herself? Just some friendless outcast my sisters took in when they should've been learning German. Yeah she's super plain. But godly and hard-working which matters more IMO

Rosamond Oliver @rosamondtheheiress

When he's a ten but he:

- Constantly criticises you

- Won't marry you despite obvious passionate regard

- Won't stop talking about the South Sea Bubble

 **Jane Eyre** Hey guys, thanks for all the messages! Sorry for going so quiet, I'm ok, been living with some dear new friends (not blood relations as far as I know!) I don't want to go into details, but I'm totally fine. Will be starting a new job soon, teaching some village urchins. Apparently you just need to be able to count and write and be a dab hand with the nit comb. My years at Lowood have prepared me amply for this.

I'm still recovering from my ordeal, and obvs need to set up my new home in the lowly cottage I've been offered (no wifi, only one servant!). If you'd like to contribute I've set up a GoPatroniseMe, link below!

www.gopatroniseme.com/poorfriendlessjane

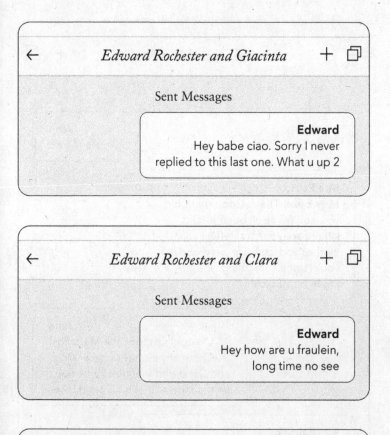

← *Edward Rochester and Giacinta* + ⎘

Sent Messages

Edward
Hey babe ciao. Sorry I never
replied to this last one. What u up 2

← *Edward Rochester and Clara* + ⎘

Sent Messages

Edward
Hey how are u fraulein,
long time no see

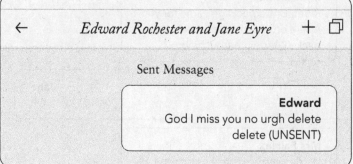

← *Edward Rochester and Jane Eyre* + ⎘

Sent Messages

Edward
God I miss you no urgh delete
delete (UNSENT)

Jane
Hey Mrs F

Mrs Fairfax
Miss Eyre!! Thank God, where did you go? We've all been frantic. Where are you? You left all your clothes and cash, we were worried you'd done something, you know . . . stupid

Jane
Oh no! I just took the MegaPost without any money or belongings and wandered friendless and alone on the moors drinking from ditches

Mrs Fairfax
Right. Btw a package came for you, Adèle opened it by mistake. A flat-pack all-terrain barouche box?

Jane
Oh

Mrs Fairfax
We donated it to Sam the footman, he's using it for his Deliveroux side hustle

Jane
Right. Anyway, I was just letting you know I'm fine. Hanging out with my new friends, just randomly ended up on their doorstep! Two sisters, and their really hot, smart God-fearing brother. If anyone asks

Mrs Fairfax
Anyone, like . . .

Jane
Just anyone at all. Let them know

Mrs Fairfax
About the really hot, smart God-fearing brother?

Jane
Yup. And that I'm living a simple but plain life, teaching the kiddos in the village school. Bless them, they are so simple and grubby. At least it's honest, no pearls or gold here. No can-canning or inflatable dart-boards, just nits, graft and gruel

Mrs Fairfax
OK

Jane
Also no bigamy so y'know. How's Thornfield? And Adèle?

Mrs Fairfax
The master sent her to school.
Figured maybe they could get the
French out of her

Jane
Oh. Is she OK there? She's not
lonely? There are some really bad
schools out there and I would know

Mrs Fairfax
It was rated 'Better than Prison'

Jane
Hmmm

Mrs Fairfax
Aren't you going to ask how he's
doing?

Jane
Still got the . . .?

Mrs Fairfax
Wife in the attic? Yup. Same old
same old, ha. The scam's over obviously but she's refusing to come
down now, I think she's started to
prefer it up there. Don't blame her
tbh, he's been a total nightmare
since you left

Mrs Fairfax
Look, I'm really sorry about what happened, I did want to tell you

Jane
Yeah a heads-up would have been helpful. Like just a little hint or two

Mrs Fairfax
We really thought we'd dropped quite a lot actually. Plus all the thumping and the occasional arson. You honestly didn't get it?

Jane
Curiosity was specifically ruled out in the job description

Mrs Fairfax
Yes I remember

Jane
OK cool well great to catch up, g2g do more nit-combing and hang out with the hot God-fearing brother, it's weird how he's so handsome and yet also so unworldly

Jane
Should anyone ask

From: admin@inheritancehunter.com
To: Jane Eyre (eyrethatIbreathe@frooglemail.com)
Date: Today at 13:15
Subject: Blood Relation

Dear Miss Eyre,

We have written a number of times to inform you of the sad death of your uncle (by blood) John Eyre, and have yet to receive a response. Is it possible our communications are being deposited in your tinned meat folder? He has left you a fortune of twenty thousand pounds. Please get in touch to claim your inheritance at your earliest convenience.

Yours,
Samuel Briggs
www.inheritancehunter.com

We find any inheritance!

This message has been flagged as TINNED MEAT

Morton Village School

We're pleased to welcome back all our boys and girls for the start of spring term!

We're pleased to say we have been rated by OFSTINC as 'About as Bad as a Workhouse'! Very exciting for us. Here is the daily timetable for the rest of the week:

5am Prayers
6am Emergency typhus first-aid drills
7am Nit-combing
8am Abacus
11am Gruel
12pm More typhus drills
1pm Lecture by Reverend Rivers on the missions, 3 to 4 hours
What time remains: Watercolours with Miss Eyre

Remember everyone that next Friday is 'dress up like a medieval peasant day'. Please have your costumes ready and bring tuppence for the bake sale.

See you soon,
Miss Eyre
Head Mistress (also Deputy Head, Head of English, Mathematics, Crafts, Watercolours, Administrator and School Nurse)

The forum for tutors and governesses

Forum private messages between: 2ndMrsDeWinter and PlainJane

2ndMrsDeWinter Hey babe, how's it going? Saw you reactivated your account!

PlainJane Yeah, I've gone back into teaching . . . Village school this time. SO MANY NITS my God

2ndMrsDeWinter It's tough out there. So lucky I've got my hubby now and all his vast riches. He's almost completely perfect

PlainJane Almost?

2ndMrsDeWinter Well, everyone has baggage don't they?

PlainJane I guess. Sometimes it's too much though

2ndMrsDeWinter I dunno, it's amazing what you can forgive, if you really love someone

PlainJane Really??

2ndMrsDeWinter Oh absolutely babe, so long as it's not something totally awful. 'Totally awful' is completely subjective as well IMO. Forgive and forget I say. Seize the day!

2ndMrsDeWinter Helps if he is minted NGL

PlainJane Thanks babe, that's super helpful xxx

From: admin@inheritancehunter.com
To: St John Rivers (stjohnrivers@mortonparish.com)
Date: Today at 14:12
Subject: Eyre inheritance

Dear Mr Rivers,

Further to our correspondence informing you of the death of your uncle, John Eyre, we write to ask for your assistance in tracing his sole heir (the Eyre heir, if you will, haha. Our apologies), your long-lost cousin. Although it seems an extraordinary coincidence, we have reason to believe she may currently be residing with your sisters at Marsh End Cottage?

We know very little of her, only that she is extremely plain, was brought up traumatically by her aunt Mrs Reed, educated at Lowood School, worked for Edward Rochester at Thornfield Hall, nearly married him until discovering he had a secret wife in the attic the whole time, and then wandered friendless and alone on the moors. As you can imagine, it's not a lot to go on.

Any assistance you can provide would be greatly appreciated. Just to confirm, we checked and he didn't leave you or your sisters anything, something about a misunderstanding over a trading Ponzi scheme?

Yours,
Samuel Briggs
www.inheritancehunter.com

We find any inheritance!

St John
What r u up to?

Jane
Studying my books, improving myself

St John
Painting?

Jane
From time to time yeah

St John
Signing your name on the paintings?

Jane
🙁 Sometimes

St John
Your name Jane Elliot? That's what you said it was, right? When you randomly turned up on our door-step by complete coincidence

Jane
Eh – yeah, sure. Why?

St John
Does this Witter account mean
anything to you – @plainjane?

Jane
What's going on SJ?

St John
Look I'm going to forward you an
e-missive I just received. Have a
look at it?

Jane
Oh

Jane
Wow

Jane
OMG you're saying we are
COUSINS? By blood?

Jane
What a total and unforeseen
coincidence

St John
If you're Jane Eyre not Jane Elliot
as you said, then yes, we are cousins, and you've also inherited
twenty grand from our uncle

Jane
I have first cousins and also a rich
uncle from Madeira??? Who knew?

St John
Err the missive didn't mention
Madeira

Jane
Ehh just guessing. Quick let's tell
the girls the good news

St John, Diana, Mary, Jane

Diana
So just to get this straight, it was a total coincidence? It just happened to be our doorstep you wandered to? And now it turns out we're cousins?

Jane
Yup. Weird, huh?

Mary
It is weird, yes

Jane
Weirder things have happened. Trust me, I know. Anyway, let's focus on the positives, we're rich! No more governessing! Frog-free shoes!

Diana
And you're really sure about sharing the money? It seems a bit much, we were disinherited after all!

Jane
I could not possibly live with myself if I didn't share it. Also twenty is really easy to divide by four, even the village urchins could do that sum!

St John
Well your timing couldn't be better, I have quite an expensive but worthy project coming up 🙏

Jane Eyre So delighted that I am now an heiress! And to find out that my kind friends the Rivers are actually my first cousins, after I totally coinciden-tally wandered the moors and ended up on their exact doorstop! I know, unbelievable eh! Baking Christmas cakes for Diana and Mary's return from governessing right now. Now that I've generously shared my wealth with them, they have no need to teach the spoiled children of the bourgeoisie!

St John Rivers Yes cakes are all very well but think of the sugar content, an egg-white omelette would be better. Also don't neglect your studies and good works Jane

Jane Eyre 💀 Merry Christmas to you too SJ

Mr Brocklehurst I'm sorry but this is all totally unbelievable. The sort of thing you'd expect to find in a fantastical novel aimed at credulous women. Sad to see your childhood lies continued into adult life Jane!

Jane Eyre Look shut up, it's what happened OK??? Don't need negative trolls who have been in prison for child neglect so am blocking you

St John's Indian Adventure

Hi all, St John here! As many of you know, I've been busy learning Hindustani recently. You've probably been wondering why – SURPRISE, I'm going to India!! Planning to spread God's word to the savages there. It's a tough job but someone has to do it and I've never been one to shirk a call. And NO I won't be drinking cocktails on the beach in Goa, I'm just going there because they are in need of godly instruction. I may sample some local concoctions but simply out of respect for custom.

Anyway I need to raise ten grand travelling expenses so do give generously.

Still looking for a missionary-wife/travelling companion also, so hit me up if you know anyone. Doesn't matter what they are like as long as godly.

Comment /TessDurbeyfield Would you take me? I'm extremely sturdy and can carry two sheep at a time

> **Reply by /StJohnRivers** Maybe, as long as there's no scandal in your past? Illegitimate child, love affair, murder conviction etc?

> **Reply by /TessDurbeyfield** Oh well, it was worth a shot

Comment /JaneEyre Oh! I thought you were going to use the cash to feed the hungry locals or something, wow

Judgement-free advice for those concerned they may be committing an impropriety

AIAF for insistent proposal?

Posted by **StJohnSaves**

Am I (M29) At Fault for trying to force my cousin (F19) to marry me and go to India with me as my missionary-wife? She's keen to come but doesn't want to get married and I just think that's really inappropriate for a man of God. I mean who would believe a man could travel with his own first cousin and not get up to anything? Totally nuts but she won't be persuaded. Any tips?

Comment /EdmundBertram Go for it mate, nothing like a first-cousin wife, makes Christmas very easy

St John
If you don't come to India it's
because you hate Jesus

Jane
OK wow

St John
Are you worried about dysentery
or something?

Jane
I survived near-starvation for ten
years followed by Lowood School,
I'm pretty sure I'd cope. Like I said
I'll come, I just can't marry you.
Anyway, aren't you in love with
Rosamond Oliver?

St John
Rosamond who? I don't know who
you mean. And even if I did and I was
in love with her, it would be ungodly
to give into such base desires

Jane
Maybe you should ask her to go, St
John

St John
HAHAHA Rosamond roughing it, hilarious. She wouldn't be able to plug in her RingletKing. She's far too beautiful and precious to consider taking with me. Look, are you in love with someone else or something? I just can't think why else you wouldn't be up for this

Jane
Can't I come as your bag-handler or something? I'm told I'm very good at impersonating a hat-stand

St John
No, we have to be married. It's for Jesus. If you don't come you're going to Hell

Jane
Look, you're a nice guy SJ, but this is a bit much. I don't think I love you. You've got great hair, but I don't think that's always enough

St John
DUH I don't love you either obvs, you are so plain and waifish, but it doesn't matter! All that matters is whether you love Jesus!!!

From: progress@duolingo.com
To: Jane Eyre (eyrethatIbreathe@frooglemail.com)
Date: Today at 15:35
Subject: Repair your streak!

Dear Jane,

Warning! your ten-day streak on Duolingo Hindustani is at risk –
secure it now

Jane, Diana, Mary

Diana
So he won't let you go to India just as his cousin or helpmeet, only as his wife?

Jane
Yup

Mary
That seems . . . weird

Diana
He's my brother and I love him but HONESTLY

Mary
And he still wants to marry you even though you already gave him his share of the cash? Thank you so much for that btw, another month of governessing would have killed me, I have a morbid fear of frogs

Jane
Yeah he wants to marry me

Diana
But he doesn't love you?

Jane
Nope. I mean I am very plain

Diana
Not at all, you're beautiful babe

Mary
Inside and out

Jane
Aw you guys 💕

Diana
Also I think you would be dead in seconds in India. With your cruel upbringing and weakness of constitution

Jane
Why does everyone keep saying that? Do you know the survival rate for kids at boarding school in this country – I'm in the top 1 per cent!

Mary
But you don't love him, right?

Jane
No. But he says if I don't go I'm making Baby Jesus cry

Mary
Well let's not listen to the Reverend Judgerson on this one

Diana
Once he told me if I didn't iron my socks it would make Baby Jesus cry

Mary
Some people just want to be miserable, like he could be married to a beautiful and bubbly heiress right now but no, he'd rather catch cholera at a Full Moon party

Judgement-free advice for those concerned they may be committing an impropriety

AIAF for refusing loveless marriage?

Posted by: Eyretospare

Am I (F19) At Fault for hesitating to marry my first cousin (M29), who clearly doesn't love me and only wants me to go with him to India to help him be a missionary? I've said I'll go as a Gap Year volunteer and just be mates/cousins/even could pretend to be his sister but he's not keen. He's handsome and all (hair of a Greek God) but I'm still in love with my grumpy boss (M39, married, balding, it's complicated) and my cousin is in love with a local heiress (F19, giggly).

I don't think I'm AF but cousin is being really mardy with me and keeps reminding me how plain I am and how this is God's will. I've already given him 5k of my inheritance, you'd think that would make him happy?

Comment /Sleazydoesit Talk about missionary position LOL

Reply by /Eyretospare Oh FFS

Jane Eyre
@plainjane
Bio: Educator, artist, world traveller, fire safety officer, emergency trauma nurse, extreme survivalist, philanthropist. Working on my memoir MOOR MONEY MOOR PROBLEMS

Jane Eyre @plainjane

Guys you won't believe this. Another incredible happening. So there I was last night, valiantly attempting not to marry my hot, smart, religious-maniac first cousin and go to India with him where I would surely die of disease or upheaval, and I hear a strange sound (THREAD)

Jane Eyre @plainjane

At first I'm like – is it an urchin? A wandering cow? Our simple peasant servant Hannah watching Love Hamlet again?

Jane Eyre @plainjane

But no. It's a voice I recognise. A voice I love

Jane Eyre @plainjane

It's yelling 'Jane, Jane!'

Jane Eyre @plainjane

Jane is my name, if you can't tell

Jane Eyre @plainjane

I'm like: WTF. I ask my cousin, can he hear it but no. Just me

Jane Eyre @plainjane

So I shout back I AM COMING. As you do

Jane Eyre @plainjane

Which makes cousin look at me like I'm weird

Jane Eyre @plainjane

Let's just say, I don't think he has ever heard a woman utter that phrase before 😌

Jane Eyre @plainjane

Immediately I set out on a long journey. I don't mind being friendless on the moors as we know but it was a bit triggering to once again be at the mercy of the weather. Luckily this time I managed not to leave my bag on the MegaPost and was soon back in my old neighbourhood

Jane Eyre @plainjane

I set off walking the two miles towards Thornfield, my former home. What can I say, public transport is a disgrace in this part of the world, and I boycott Buber (the barouche-sharing company) out of principle

Jane Eyre @plainjane

As I approached I saw it – Thornfield Hall had burned to the ground! Just a blackened ruin echoing with the joys of days past. Where were the people I loved? Where was the floral arch? The gins in cans?

Jane Eyre @plainjane

I fled to a nearby Spoons and ordered a restorative gin (not in can but only tuppence, not bad). YES I know people are boycotting the chain but we must think of the poor, also Tuesday night is curry night

Jane Eyre @plainjane

Landlord says yep there was a terrible fire. Whole place went up. Mentions 'the late Mr Rochester' and I almost pass out

Jane Eyre @plainjane

Turns out he meant the *father* of my Mr R. You'd think people could be more specific.

But anyway. Mine did get caught in the fire, he's still alive but badly injured. Blind and lost a hand trying to save his wife who started the blaze (I did warn them about this, health and safety was sadly neglected in that house).

Jane Eyre @plainjane

He's at his secondary mansion in the woods it turns out, Ferndean. I'm sitting here right now trying to find out how to get to him

Jane Eyre @plainjane

Anyway, long story short I heard the ACTUAL voice of my beloved ex-fiancé, from HUNDREDS of MILES AWAY at the EXACT moment he must have cried out to me. Can you explain this??

@mrbrocklehurst

I'm sorry but this is FAKE NEWS. Bad enough you expect us to believe you randomly stumbled on your long-lost first cousins, but now you're hearing voices? Bet you just sat on your phone or something

@plainjane

Wow Mr B, not got much to do except stalk me across multiple platforms eh? What is it, hate to see a former student survive your reign of starvation and tyranny and become an independent heiress? How else do you explain what happened except divine intervention or magic, eh?

Archive files from Alexa device, Ferndean Manor

00:03

Alexa stop calling Jane, I said DON'T call Jane, for God's sake bloody thing why did I let Adèle talk me into it Mrs F Mrs F come and turn this off will you

Deadly Fire at Thornfield Hall

A terrible fire has broken out at Thornfield Hall, home to local disgraced landowner Edward Rochester (39) and his wife, Bertha (44, presumed deceased, now deceased).

All inhabitants were saved with the exception of Bertha Rochester, née Mason, whom we previously reported dead in a tragic canoeing accident. Apparently she is really dead this time.

Mr Rochester issued the following statement following the blaze:

'RIP my beautiful wife, who definitely is dead this time, very sad. I hope the Reassured Gentlemen insurance company will finally see fit to pay out the life insurance monies, which would be helpful now my primary mansion has burned down.'

Mr Rochester is reported to be grievously injured. In a Zoom call with this newspaper, he wore a mask and sat in darkness, stating,

'Don't look at me, I'm hideously deformed!! My former glory is all cut down, how shall anyone ever love me again?'

We were unable to obtain independent verification of the extent of his injuries, but enquiries with EyesRUs in London confirmed that Mr Rochester is currently a patient.

Investigations into the cause of the inferno are pending, but it is believed to have started in the attic, where a large quantity of flammable materials were being stored (gins in cans, sudoku books and a surprising quantity of expertly hemmed curtains).

Whilst we were unable to obtain footage of the disaster, a talented local artist provided us with an impression of events as they unfolded.

www.frooglemaps.com

Directions to Ferndean:

1. Walk to Millcote

2. Hire barouche or hail one via Buber

3. Walk 6 miles through the woods

The forum for tutors and governesses

Forum private messages between: PlainJane and 2ndMrsDeWinter

PlainJane OMG, you won't believe what's been going on. So the first wife actually is dead now

2ndMrsDeWinter He finally killed her? Thank God, I'm so glad Max just got on and did it the first time around, all this attic hiding is just messy

PlainJane What??? No she died accidentally in a fire she set. Are you saying . . .??

2ndMrsDeWinter Look there were really good reasons, she was a total floozy. And like really taunting you know? So glad Max is free from her evil spell. And yours is too! Yay, wedding bells????

PlainJane Well I don't know. The whole hiding her in the attic thing I feel is not good, even if it was her idea, plus the attempted bigamy and all. Some red flags there maybe

2ndMrsDeWinter At least he got around to tidying up the loose ends eventually

PlainJane He hasn't actually killed her, just to be clear! It was a tragic accident. If only I'd been there in my capacity as fire-safety officer

2ndMrsDeWinter Riiiiiight

PlainJane But you think we could still have a future together? You're happy right?

2ndMrsDeWinter Totally!! We almost never think about the ex now. There was some admin stuff to sort out, but apart from that, fine. And you know, we had the fire our end also. Such a nightmare! Everything smells of smoke

PlainJane And your housekeeper died?

2ndMrsDeWinter Well between you and me that was kind of a blessing. Just wish she'd done it without scorching my Prada

PlainJane No judgement from other people though about all the murder and that?

2ndMrsDeWinter Oh, hardly anyone knows, he managed to hush the whole thing up. LOL don't tell anyone

PlainJane I think the attic thing is pretty much out in the open now. So you think I should go for it? Marry him this time?

2ndMrsDeWinter Absolutely! What are you, like 19? When you get to our age you have to make compromises babe. Everyone has flaws and tiny things like bigamy or murder can totes be overlooked. Helps if he's minted xxx

PlainJane Thanks this has been really helpful xxx

Jane
Don't tell him I'm here ok?

Mrs Fairfax
What am I supposed to say?? It's
not like he won't notice

Jane
Tell him I'm a hat-stand

Mrs Fairfax
OK. I don't really get why though.
He's going to be thrilled you're here

Jane
It's more romantic this way. Stick
some coats on me and we'll wait till
he notices

Mrs Fairfax
This is really weird

Jane
Then when he walks past I'll hold out
the ring. Maybe he can make out its
faint glint in the midst of his surround-
ing darkness. Or just bump into it

Mrs Fairfax
You know he's not actually blind right? I think there's been some confusing reports in the papers and he wanted to claim more on the insurance. He just needs varifocals

Jane
My poor broken darling, I shall nurse him back to God's light

Mrs Fairfax
😟 You two are really made for each other

The dating site for those who shun romantic debasement in favour of pious practicality

St John Rivers, 29. Vicar seeks wife for Indian trip. Love is not necessary as long as you have a robust condition to deal with the heat, disease, and uprisings. Going in like three weeks so need to sort this quick so you can get your jabs and visa. Accidental death waiver will also be required.

Eliza Reed, 24. Seeking a godly marriage where I can pray in peace and get away from my strumpet sister. Brother recently died of dissipation and I just want out.

Forum private messages between: StJohn and Eliza

StJohn	Hey gurl. Are you a good work because I would like to do you
Eliza	😍
StJohn	Ever been to India?
Eliza	Go on . . .

Jane Rochester
@plainjane
Bio: Jane Rochester @plainjane Former educator, artist, world traveller, now wife to @edwardrochester. Working on my memoir (DM me for info)

Jane Eyre @plainjane

Witter, I married him! #putaringonit #mrsrochester Grumpy ex-boss that is. Not hot first cousin

 @edwardrochester
You said he wasn't hot!!

 @plainjane

Edward
Jane

Edward
Jane

Edward
Jane

Edward
Will you bring me up the paper and a cup of tea

Jane
You can't get it yourself? Or like ask one of the servants? Since I'm no longer your employee and all

Edward
Servants?? I hardly have any now I'm so reduced in the world

Jane
Um we still have four, that's a 2:1 ratio. Know how many I had in my lowly cottage? Just one, that's right. Imagine living with just one servant. Had to make my own gnocchi and everything

Edward
I'm blind and I lost a hand 😟

Jane
Ed you broke a nail and you need varifocals because you are old enough to be my dad, that's all

Edward
BUT I'M DYING

Edward
It's bad enough I had to move to my secondary mansion and now I can't even get a cup of tea

Jane
I'm the one who's preggers mate. When Adèle comes home for the holidays she can make you tea

From: appointments@eyesrus.com
To: Edward Rochester (edwardrochesteresq@thornfieldhall.com)
Date: Today at 12:59
Subject: Your appointment with EyesRUs is scheduled for –
Tuesday at 11am

Dear Mr Rochester,

We are pleased to hear of the improvement in your symptoms and
look forward to seeing you for a follow-up appointment soon.

Please allow plenty of time to get to London (three days at least) and
do not attend if you have any symptoms of typhus.

From: masonjar@frooglemail.com
To: edwardrochesteresq@thornfieldhall.com
Date: Today at 16:41
Subject: Blender??

Heyyy Eddy,

Yesssss we finally did it!! Fake death, achievement unlocked!! Thanks for your help with the fire, sorry about the house (and the whole blindness/maiming thing, though I can't help thinking you were exaggerating there tbh, you always were a bit dramatic about papercuts etc, typical man!) I really did mean to keep it contained to the attic but those curtains turned out to be super flammable, and after all those months of seclusion Grace had made quite a pile of them.

Look, I know I said I'd go quietly in return for making off with all the life insurance money, but just had one more question. Have you any idea what happened to the blender in the fire? Would be nice to have some smoothies out here, maybe with a dash of gin in them LOL.

Weather is lovely in Jamaica, hope you are happy with your child-bride.

Bertha xx

From: george@worthytomes.com
To: masonjar@frooglemail.com
Date: Today at 12:23
Subject: Your submission

Dear Miss Mertha Bason (what an unusual name btw!),

Thank you for the submission of your memoir *Cached in the Attic:
from hiding yourself to finding yourself*. We are very excited about
this story of rising above the drudgery of a toxic marriage and we
think this will really appeal to our readership of put-upon women. I'm
pleased to offer you an advance of three hundred guineas, and am
of course happy to publish completely anonymously as requested.
We can also accede to your rather unusual request of a lifetime
supply of Pot Noodles in lieu of royalties.

Yours,
George Lewis (Esq)
Publishing Director, Worthy Tomes Ltd

From: george@worthytomes.com
To: eyrethatibreathe@frooglemail.com
Date: Today at 12:48
Subject: Your submission

Dear Mrs Jane Rochester,

Thank you for the submission of your memoir *FRIENDLESS – a governess's guide to marrying up, surviving bigamy, and finding happiness*. As we unfortunately had to turn down your guide to moors survival *Moor Money Moor Problems*, due to legal doubts about its veracity, we were pleased to see another manuscript from you and would be happy to offer you a publishing contract. Have you considered becoming a Mummy Spinstagrammer btw? Just a thought.

Yours,
George Lewis (Esq)
Publishing Director, Worthy Tomes Ltd

The forum for tutors and governesses

**Forum private messages between: PlainJane and
2ndMrsDeWinter**

PlainJane Do you ever get sick of people saying, oh no your husband
is a gaslighter, he still murdered his first wife even if she did kind of
deserve it, he's a bad person, blah blah blah?

2ndMrsDeWinter God yeah all the time

PlainJane I mean mine didn't even kill his wife – he tried to save her
life! – but still getting a lot of judgement about the attic thing. Like what
else was he supposed to do? And he only tried to marry me biga-
mously because he was so in love. It's romantic when you think about
it.

PlainJane Anyway g2g, Eddy can't find the paper again even though
it's in his lap. I guess that's what you get for marrying someone old
enough to be your dad!

2ndMrsDeWinter You're lucky you had that backup mansion, our
stupid builders can't seem to renovate a sixty-bed house in less than a
year. Currently living a hellish hand-to-mouth existence on the Riviera,
just a small villa between the two of us

PlainJane Thinking of you hun xxx

- Fin -

Glossary

---shire: Contrary to certain scurrilous rumours, all of the events relayed in the above tome are true occurrences, that definitely actually happened. Therefore, we have taken steps to conceal the locations involved, as is customary in contemporary so-called 'fiction'

AIAF: A popular forum for those concerned they may have committed an impropriety. If you fear you may have slighted a relative, snubbed a member of the landed gentry or been curt to your housemaid, a friendly community of non-judgemental individuals are on hand to answer your query: Am I At Fault?

ClickClock, Froogle, Witter, Spinstergram: sites of social intercourse bearing no relation to any similar-sounding equivalents

Deliveroux: Avoid awkward dinner party mix-ups with this fast and efficient meal delivery service! A fleet of footmen can deliver to your door in mere moments, using a newly rolled-out efficient barouche-box express service

Madeiran Trading Company: A vast and impressively lucrative trading conglomerate

OFSTINC: The Office for Standards in Children's Incarceration, ensuring suspiciously waifish and friendless youngsters are housed in only the most spartan and improving of environments

Tinned Meat: Unwanted or robot-generated missives

Acknowledgements

Our most humble and sincere thanks . . .

to our editor Sorcha Rose, designer Sofia Hericson, artist Amy Batley, production controller Claudette Morris, marketer Melissa Grierson, publicist Alara Delfosse and copy editor Jacqui Lewis, and everyone at Hodder who worked on this book – we've had so much fun putting it together. Thanks also to Sara Adams and Bea Fitzgerald for their help at the start

to Juliet Mushens and Diana Beaumont, agents extraordinaire

to our families and friends for their support, and for once again enduring our constant quoting and frequently terrible, extremely niche puns

and, of course, to Charlotte Brontë for writing a wonderful book – though we're pretty sure she would absolutely hate this one and would probably sue . . .

Claire and Sarah

Elizabeth Bennet has politely declined your friend request and asks that you do not slide into her DMs again.

Have you ever wondered what Austen's most famous couple might be like if it played out online? Well, here is the story in full

. . .

Out now.